Beauty and the Chief

By

ALYSIA S. KNIGHT

Heart Dreams
PRESS

Beauty and the Chief
By Alysia S. Knight
Published by Heart Dreams Press
Copyright © 2015 Alysia S. Knight
Cover design: by Kelli Ann Morgan @
www.inspirecreativeservices.com

The views expressed within this work are the sole responsibility of the author and do not represent Heart Dreams Press or any of its affiliates.

This is a work of fiction. Names, characters, place and events are product of the author's imagination. Any similarities to actual persons, living or dead, business establishments or events are purely coincidental.

ISBN:1942000030
ISBN-13:978-1-94200003-7

Also available from
Alysia S. Knight

Letting Love Win

ଓଞ୍ଚ

Past To Die For

ଓଞ୍ଚ

Temperature Rising

ଓଞ୍ଚ

Kare for Me

ଓଞ୍ଚ

Blind Witness

ଓଞ୍ଚ

Trail to Her Heart

ଓଞ୍ଚ

His Governess

To all those who have had faith in me.

Alysia S. Knight

Chapter One

"That's my girl. Ready for your walk?" Jillian struggled to snap the leash to the excited yellow Lab's collar. "Down," she reprimanded with a smile, while dodging the wet tongue. "Sit. That's a good girl." She stroked the dog's honey-white fur which was only a couple shades lighter than the hair that hung in a ponytail halfway down her back.

The instant the door opened, the Lab lunged forward. At thirteen months old, Abby didn't look much like a puppy anymore. Her head reached Jillian's thigh and, even though she still had the leanness of youth, it took quite a bit of Jillian's strength to hold back the eighty pounds of four-legged muscle.

"Abby stay, sit," Jillian ordered as she struggled to lock the door. Turning from the lighted porch, she peered into the misty darkness common to the coast this time of year. "Let's make this fast tonight. We're late." Jillian suppressed a shudder, grateful for the soft comfort of her well-worn sweat suit.

Starting out on a slow jog, they made it through the security gate and across the street to the park. Jillian smiled at the dog keeping stride beside her. Getting Abby was one of the best decisions she'd ever made in her life. She needed the companionship, and Abby was a wonderful dog;

smart and full of love. A little too lively and liked to chew on things, but she was still young. Their walks and runs were especially satisfying now that they were no longer pulling matches. The thought hardly crossed her mind when Abby lunged forward, tugging Jillian off the path.

"Abby, heel," Jillian commanded breathlessly but, for once, the dog totally ignored her, dragging her over the slippery grass. "Abby!" The leash dug into her hand. To Jillian's relief, Abby stopped, looking back a split second before returning her gaze to the fog.

Apprehension filled Jillian as she ran her hand over the dog's rigid body. Suddenly, the night felt too black, too quiet. Why am I out here this late? "This isn't smart, Jillian, you know better." The words said aloud died in the fog. She had always made it a practice never to go out running alone after dark, even with Abby, but tonight she'd worked late, trying to please a customer and then she had stopped at the store for milk, and her car wouldn't start when she came out. Her brain was rambling, she realized.

She was frightened.

"Let's head back. It's been a long day," she said softly as a shiver ran through her body. She gave a light tug on the leash. Abby turned to follow but only made it a few steps.

A muffled whimpering snaked out of the mist.

Abby spun, jerking Jillian around. Her body rigid, she growled into the darkness.

"Abby, what is it?" Her voice went up several octaves. Not knowing what the sound was, but the fact that she had only heard Abby growl playfully before, frightened her.

Abby's lunge came so fast it pulled Jillian off her feet, ripping the leash from her hand. The park light glistened off the golden coat just before the dog disappeared between two trees. "Abby!" She sprang after her dog without a thought. A branch appeared out of the mist striking her across her face. Jillian slowed her pace an instant before she stumbled into a small, secluded clearing.

Abby's growl, joined by a muffled curse, caused Jillian to turn. A scream broke from her lips at the same time an agonized whine pierced the air. The mist-diffused streetlights were some distance away, but there was still enough light to define the sharp, metal edge of a knife before the dark figure turned to her. Jillian stumbled back into a picnic table. Going down, she hit the ground only a second before a monstrous hand snaked out, locked in her hair, and hauled her up.

Hot breath assaulted her face. Bulging skin and deformed features loomed at her. It took a second to realize that only the dark, wild eyes were real.

"Beauty." The word dragged out in caressing syllables. "Scream, Beauty, scream." The harsh words taunted her – she was indeed screaming. Jillian lashed out. Her hand contacted with the spongy rubber of a grotesque mask. Digging her fingers in, she struggled and fought but couldn't do any damage to the face beneath.

A deep-throated laugh rumbled in her face. Jillian felt the attacker's excitement as he pulled her around by the hair and forced her down to the table, pinning her with his heavy body. "Love me, beauty, love me."

"No!" Jillian's denial erupted in a pained gasp.

With his savage hiss, she caught sight of the knife coming at her.

"No!" She kicked out, missing with her foot, but her knee connected with the soft tissue of his thigh. With a grunt, the hand holding the knife came down, hard knuckles connecting with her cheek instead of cold, sharp metal.

Lights flashed in front of her eyes as her body was jerked around like a rag doll. Jillian could no longer move to stop the assault.

"Beauty." The word rasped against her cheek.

A snarl filled the air that didn't come from the beast. A

deep-throated cry echoed in Jillian's foggy mind and morphed into the wail of a siren. Released, she dropped. Her fall ended with the hard impact on the ground.

Through the fog, voices joined the sirens. Jillian struggled to move. Her hand bumped soft fur. She received a faint whine.

"Abby," Jillian's whisper flooded with tears. She sank her face into the golden coat, ignoring the sticky wetness on her cheek. She felt the damp tongue touch her fingers, as the lights and voices surrounded her.

Chapter Two

Police Chief Mark Richards hunched over the file open on his desk. The last two months, it had become a nightly routine. Praying that, if he looked long enough, he'd find some shred of evidence that would give them a lead to go on. Unfortunately, he knew the reports inside out and there was nothing. The only similarity was that a stab wound to the heart had killed the two women.

Leaning back in the chair, he pressed his thumb and forefinger to the bridge of his nose. He should go home and get some rest. Mrs. Morris, his housekeeper, would've long since left his dinner in the fridge, where it would be waiting to be warmed up. Jordan, his ten-year-old son, was at a movie with friends. He smiled at the thought of Jordan, the best part of his life.

Pushing on the floor with one foot, he turned his chair to the window. The fog was thick tonight. The perfect scene from a horror movie, but this was no movie. The villain was real and lurking in his city. Preying on young, beautiful women he had sworn to protect.

"Chief, we got lucky." Edward Samuelson's voice came through the office door behind him. "It looks like he struck again."

A hiss broke from Mark's lips as he spun his chair

toward the door to the burly officer, his second in command, and friend. "What do you mean, lucky?" Mark's words were brusque. He didn't ask what Edward referred to.

"The victim's alive, and we have a witness."

Mark was out of his chair, across the room and snagging his raincoat from the rack in one second flat.

Edward fell into step beside him, well used to working this way. "The call came in from Roseland Park, not five minutes ago. They're combing the area now." He continued to give details.

Roseland Park, not even a mile from his home. A quiet, beautiful park where he'd taken his son since Jordan was a baby.

Lights and policemen flooded the area as Mark pulled his car to a screeching halt. The single red flashing light on top of his car blended with the myriad of others. To one side, an ambulance was being closed up. The Chief of Detectives came toward them flipping through pages of a small notebook.

"Mark."

"Andrew, what have we got?" Mark looked over the scene.

"A call came in. A lady heard screaming in the park. Luckily, we had a unit about three blocks away. Our suspect fled. We have teams searching the neighborhoods for him."

"We know it was a man?" Mark cut in.

The police captain nodded. "The witness gave a partial: male, approximately six feet, wearing a baggy dark sweater or sweatshirt. The rest is kind of shaky. She's in shock." He led the way to the crime scene. "It appears our witness was out jogging with her dog and interrupted the killer. He then went after her and the dog got in the way. We have this." He motioned to a rubber mask in an evidence bag. "Our witness managed to pull it off in the struggle. And, you ought to like this." He held out a bag containing a knife with a six-inch blade. Fresh blood marked the steel and the bag.

"Maybe it is our turn to be lucky." Mark turned toward the ambulance pulling away. "I want photos of every inch of the area, and go over it more thoroughly than with a fine tooth comb."

"Knew you would. It's already in progress," Detective Andrew Hamilton assured.

"Good, what can you tell me about the victims?"

"In the ambulance, we have a female. Caucasian. About twenty-two years old. Looks like he was following his MO, but either because the jogger and the dog interrupted him or possibly the girl struggled, he missed his mark. One stab wound to the chest. Paramedics are still trying to get her stable. They weren't sure if it nicked the heart, but appears there's blood in the lungs. Can't give us odds on whether she'll survive or not, but at least she has a chance."

"That's more than any of the others have had so far," Mark reminded grimly. "Do we have a name?"

"No ID as yet."

"Her name is Sandra." The voice was faint, unsteady.

Mark turned. "You know her?" He assessed the woman who stood before him wrapped in a blanket from a cruiser. She was slightly taller than average, between five foot seven and five eight. Her hair was a mixture of gold and light blonde. At one time that night, it would have been pulled back into a ponytail, but now the better part of it had been ripped free to tangle around her face. Floodlights glistened off the tears in her blue eyes, which were bright with fear.

She winced slightly as she nodded her head, struggling to swallow. "Not well. She works at Delaney's Market. We always spoke. She's very nice. Was the employee of the month last month, had her picture in the newspaper. She saved a little boy in the store that choked on a piece of candy. I don't know her last name."

Mark recognized the rambling tendencies as a sign of shock.

"Miss Taylor, this is Police Chief Richards," Detective Hamilton said.

There was another slight grimace as she made a motion to nod her head.

"Chief, Jillian Taylor."

Mark stepped forward. The woman appeared unsteady on her feet. Close up, he noticed a faint redness on her left cheek. The suspect was probably right-handed. He made a mental note. Mark didn't notice the heavy silence in the air until it was broken by one of the officers calling Andrew's attention.

"I'll go with Hamilton." Edward turned, going after the detective. The woman's eyes followed the two men in the direction of a picnic table and the large area cordoned off with yellow police tape. Noticeable shudders ran through her body as she hugged the blanket tighter around her.

"Why don't we move over here?" Placing a hand on her elbow, he directed her to a nearby police car. From Mark's six foot two height, the woman at his side seemed small. Another shudder shook her, pulling at something deep within him. An urge to shelter her hit him. He shoved the thought away. He was tired. Relieved, when he reached the car, he opened the front door, motioning for her to sit.

"Does the police chief always handle investigations?" Jillian Taylor looked up at him.

"In this case, yes. Besides, we're not such big a city that I don't get involved." He forced a smile. Reassurance was what she was seeking.

Sliding his hand into his pocket, he pushed the button on the small recorder he had placed there before leaving the car. Squatting down in front of her, he laced his fingers together. "Can you tell me what happened?"

Fear deepened in her eyes but, with a deep breath, she nodded.

The lady has courage.

"I was taking my dog, Abby, for our nightly walk." She caught back a sob. "Actually, we were jogging tonight. I was late getting home."

"So you usually don't go out this late?"

"No, normally it's around six to six thirty."

"All right. Continue." He kept his tone soft, reassuring.

"Abby stopped and started to growl. Then she broke away, and ran off into the trees. I went after her. It was probably a foolish thing to do, but I didn't think."

Mark didn't think either before laying his hand over hers, giving it a squeeze.

"There was a whine. I knew it was Abby's this time."

"This time?"

"There … there was a sound before … before Abby took off."

"Okay, so you heard Abby's whine. Was it close?"

She nodded. Her eyes filling with tears, her breath becoming ragged. "When I turned, Abby was on the ground. There was this big shadow, then it moved, and I could see a woman. Then the shadow was in front of me. It was so … it was gross. He grabbed the back of my head, pulling me toward him." Tears flooded the words now.

Mark again touched her hand to keep her grounded. "It's all right now. Take your time. He can't hurt you. You're safe." He kept his voice low and reassuring.

"He called me 'Beauty.'"

Mark couldn't hide his shock, but the woman didn't seem to notice, as she continued, "'Scream, Beauty, scream. Love me, Beauty'. I don't think I realized it was a mask until I tried to dig my nails into his face. He laughed. That was when he said, 'Love me.'"

"Love me, Beauty?" Mark asked to clarify.

She looked at him, gathering a little more composure.

"Yes. 'Love me, Beauty, Love me.'"

"That's exactly what he said?"

"Yes."

"You're doing fine, go on," he encouraged.

"We were struggling. He had a knife in his hand. He was going to kill me. That's all I could think over and over again. He was going to kill me. I tried to kick him, but he hit me, then Abby was there. I think she bit him. He was gone, and there were sirens, red lights, and police." The last few words came calmer.

"Good. Now, I want you to describe him. You said it was a man, around six feet. What kind of build?"

"I don't know, I …"

"I know it's hard, Jillian," using her first name for familiarity, "but I want you to try. He was about six feet?"

"Yes, when he breathed, his breath hit me in the face when he pushed me against the table."

"Good, that's about right for six feet. How was he built?"

"He was … he was strong, big, not really burly, but not lean like you. His muscles were not hard, but he was still strong." Shudders ran over her.

"It's all right." Again he rested a hand on hers.

"Can you tell me what he looked like? You pulled off his mask."

Instantly, her trembling multiplied, and her breathing became erratic. Her hand pulled away from his, going to her mouth to stifle a sob.

"It's all right." Breaking his cardinal rule, he put his arm around her. Her head tipped down to rest on his shoulder. He wanted to pull her closer, but fought the desire. He wished he didn't have to continue the questioning. That he could make it all go away. But for it to go away, he had to stop this monster, and to do that he had to have answers.

Wanting to protect someone had never been this

pronounced. What was it about the vulnerable look of Jillian Taylor that tore at him? He started to ease her away when the dam which had been holding back her tears broke free, letting the hot drops burn his skin all the way to his heart.

"He was going to kill her. He was going to kill me. All the blood," the woman sobbed. "So …"

Mark tightened his hold on her, letting her cry until the sobs faded, turning into muffled hiccups.

He sat her back from him. With one hand, he wiped away the tears.

"I'm sorry."

He almost smiled at her apology. "It's all right. You've earned it. I'm sorry but I have to ask you again. Can you describe him?"

"He … he was backlit." Her trembling started up again.

"Okay." He pressed on. "Let's start with his hair. If you couldn't tell what color, was it long or short?"

She shook her head. "He didn't have any hair. He was bald."

"Bald! You're positive?"

She gasped, to hold back tears, nodding again. "His –," she put her hand back to her mouth, covering her trembling chin, swallowing hard several times. "His head was awful. The scalp was rough. I felt it when the mask came free. It was scarred or something."

"All right. What about his face?"

"I didn't see his face. It was in shadows or turned down toward Abby. She attacked him. She saved me. How is she? How's Abby?"

"You don't know?"

She shook her head. "One of the policemen was going to take her to the vet."

He hadn't thought of the dog, but he wanted – needed – to do something to give her some comfort. "Wait here just a minute, and I'll find out?"

She nodded.

"You'll be all right?"

She nodded again.

Mark stood and motioned a nearby policewoman over. "Watch her."

He walked across the wet grass to his second in command. "Edward?"

"They completed the search of the surrounding area." Aggravation hung heavy in the man's voice. "No sign of our attacker. Mackey's dog had a possible scent, but it dead-ended in a driveway a block and a half away. The people in the house are gone on vacation according to a neighbor. No one saw anything, but a kid did hear a car start up just shortly after the sirens. Looks like our guy got away."

"Anyone see anything earlier?"

Edward shook his head. "The fog and mist kept most people in. The lady that called just happened to be letting in her cat when she heard the screaming. Both women are very lucky."

"Tell me about it. All right. Keep a couple patrol cars in the area tonight." Mark pulled his collar up around his neck. The mist was turning into a light rain. "Tell Stuart I want a copy of all the photos and his report on my desk as soon as possible."

"Like yesterday," Edward returned.

"I'm taking Miss Taylor to the hospital. She should be checked out. Have you heard anything on her dog? She's asking." Mark looked over to the cruiser where the woman sat huddled in the front seat.

"Hamilton said they sent it over to Mountain View. Two cuts. Hopefully not bad. That dog deserves a medal."

"Or at least a steak, cooked medium-rare. I'll see you in the morning." Mark watched the criminologists bending over the ground inside the yellow taped-off area, and offered a silent plea that there would be more clues to this maniac.

Turning, his eyes again rested on the young woman wrapped in a blanket. At least, tonight the beast didn't win. The victim was alive. They had some keys that might lead to catching this guy.

As he walked to the police car he felt his heart stir as it hadn't for a long time. One key he found very appealing. He chastened himself for the thought even as he took stock of Jillian Taylor. Her head was tilted to the side, leaning against the backrest. The light from the car illuminated her features. Dark eyelashes lowered to creamy smooth cheeks. Sweet, innocent, vulnerable, all ran through his mind as he stopped in front of her.

Longing hit him hard, making him want to reach down, and pull her up in his arms, so he could keep the dark, harsh world at bay. He didn't want pain to have any place in Jillian Taylor's life.

A quick nod to the policewoman and she moved off. Crouching down, he watched the peaceful face for a moment. He longed to brush back the lock of hair that had fallen across her cheek. Her eyes sprung open, bright, alert, but as they locked on his face, fear disappeared from the blue depths.

"You ready to go?" Mark found his voice odd to his ears, low and husky.

She didn't ask where they were going, only nodded. Her large eyes fixed on his making him wonder if she, too, felt a stirring. Reaching out a hand, he helped her to stand then released her quickly. He extended his arm indicating the direction. "This way." Again his hand found a way to her. Catching her elbow, he led her around the front of the car.

"We'll −" A flash burst in front of his eyes, cutting him off. The gasp beside him caused him to spin. He felt the contact of Jillian's body and wrapped his arms around to protect her. Looking back over his shoulder, the afterglow faded, so he could make out the solid built man with the camera up, ready for another shot.

"Clark, get that thing out of my face." In the year he'd known the reporter, the man had always gotten on his nerves.

"It's good press."

"Not tonight. And you're a reporter not a photographer." Mark cut back, not withholding his annoyance from his voice.

"Hey, I'm a man of many talents and it makes it easier if I get my own shots. I have a good eye. Tell me who this beauty is?"

At the word 'beauty,' Mark heard Jillian's little gasp. Tightening his arm, he pressed her to his side. She'd had enough tonight without facing the arrogant, pushy reporter.

"Out of my way, Clark," he pulled Jillian into step with him, as he maneuvered around the man.

"Hey, come on, Richards. What's going on down here? The public has a right to know." The man moved back into their path.

"There'll be a statement in the morning."

"It was the killer. Then who's the victim? She found the body? Did she see him?" The reporter pushed a mini recorder at them.

"Get that thing out of my face before I have you arrested," Mark growled.

"You can't. Freedom of the press. Now, what's her name?" The camera flashed again.

"Edward!" Mark released Jillian, stepping in front of her. Shielding her with his body. "You'll get your statement first thing in the morning, but for now, back off."

His second in command came running up, shouldering his way between the two men. Taking the reporter's arm, he tugged him away. "Come on, Clark. If you behave, I'll let you get a picture of Miller over there doing his thing.

Otherwise, we'll take a run around the park. Maybe you can find some other sicko out preying on young women."

"So it was the same guy. We have a serial killer on our hands." The man's excitement came through so that you could hear "good press" and "hot scoop" written all over his tone.

"Two killings don't make a serial killer."

Mark heard his second comment, knowing down inside it was wrong. They did have a serial killer – a sick mind lashing out, targeting beautiful young women. And, if they didn't find him soon, more would die.

The maniac slipped up tonight. He'd err again, and they'd get him. Opening the door of his sedan, he settled Jillian in. Her face turned away from the night, pressing into the seat. Mark closed the door to shut out the conversation behind him.

"Two, you mean the victim's still alive?" The reporter's voice was hot with excitement. "Was that the victim? Come on, give me something Samuelson."

Mark climbed in the driver's side cutting out the further comments. Edward could handle Clark.

Chapter Three

Mark started the car before looking across at the woman next to him. Her eyes were closed again. In the faint glow of the dash, he thought he could see her chin tremble. Leaning over, he caught the edge of the blanket, pulling it over and tucking it around the muddy knees of her sweat pants.

Looking up, he found himself staring into fathomless, watery blue eyes. They called to him. What was it about those eyes? So compelling. He clutched the wheel to keep his hand from going to her face again to cradle the softness.

As if conscious of his desire, her face tilted down shyly to stare at the folds of the blanket around her. Floodlights coming in from the rear window gave her an ethereal glow. She'd have the wide, innocent, doe-eyes if they had been brown instead of vivid blue. His heart leapt.

She certainly did have a powerful effect on him.

Clearing his throat, he drew her attention. "Miss Taylor, I'd like to take you to the hospital to be checked out."

Jillian shook her head. "It's not necessary. I'm not hurt – just a few bruises."

"I would feel better though if you were checked out.

You've had quite a shock." He paused a moment. "It would also be better for us. When you struggled with the man you were in direct contact. It's possible you could have skin, blood, or hair samples on you that could help."

He noticed again her chin trembling. The burning urge to take her in his arms and sweep her fears away ached in him, but he remained still in his seat.

"The officer ... tech ... he already ... my hands." Her voice and petered out to a whisper.

"I know. It's all right. I'd just like to have you checked out again." This time, he was unable to counter his reflexes, as his hand reached to squeeze her arm through the blanket. "Would you mind? I already have an investigator at the hospital."

"You'll be there too?" The words came out so sudden Mark could tell they surprised her also.

"Yes, I'll stay there with you." He gave her arm another squeeze, while telling himself that it didn't mean anything. It wasn't uncommon for victims to affix themselves to one person as their lifeline. There was no special reason that she chose him as hers. Still, a quiver of pleasure raced through him that she had.

He frowned at his next directive. "There is another thing. If we could get your jogging suit to run through the lab for smudges and ..." A tear glistened in the corner of her eye. I hate this. She's been through enough for one night.

"Of course, if we could stop at my condo. It's just at the other end of the park so I could get some other clothes." She sounded stiff, making him feel like more of an ogre.

"Certainly." He figured there'd be less contaminates there than they'd pick up at the hospital. Putting the car in gear, he drove to her condo was made with only a couple directions and the punching of the keypad to gain entry at the gate to break the silence.

The porch light glowed through the heavy fog like a

guiding beacon to a secure port. But when the young woman jumped at his touch on her elbow, Mark wondered if, after a night like this, there was any place that would make Jillian Taylor feel secure again?

She unlocked the door and stepped in, keeping her back between him and the keypad on the wall as she punched in the number deactivating the alarm.

By her instinctive caution, he could tell Jillian Taylor was normally a careful with her safety. It was just an odd sequence of events that put her in the deadly position she had been in this night. But the same could be said for about a thousand other hapless people each day. The wrong place, the wrong time, and they were in the midst of bad situations.

"I'll just go up and change." Her words broke through his thoughts. Her voice seemed stronger now in the surroundings of her own home.

"Fine, just remember not to wash."

"They ... they already."

"I'd like to have it done again." He cursed himself as her face paled, but swallowing, her shoulders straightened.

She nodded, turning the corner to the stairs, leaving him to wander around.

Stepping forward, he looked around the corner into a well-lit kitchen. Except for a glass, bowl, and spoon in the sink, it was neat and tidy. Either she hadn't had dinner yet this evening, or she stopped on the way home. He guessed the former. Sitting off to the side, in the corner of the floor, were two large metal bowls on a mat. One contained water while the other remained empty, waiting.

Another step took him into the large, open living area. To his right, light spilt in from the opening over the kitchen counter into the dining room, or what would be the dining room. For Jillian, the room contained a large antique roll top desk holding a computer and a small stack of papers.

On the other wall was a drafting table with several

rolls of paper and an assortment of pens, pencils, and other tools laid out around the top. There was no dining table so Jillian either did little entertaining or no more than could fit at her small table in the kitchen.

He turned to the main living area. The room spoke of sheer elegance but, at the same time, was warm, inviting and comfortable. No contemporary, modern stuff, he thought with pleasure. Rich cherry wood tables and entertainment cabinet, rose and blue print couch, and blue chairs all tied together with a large oriental area rug centered in front of the fireplace. All in all, it was classy, not overly feminine so it would leave a man feeling uncomfortable in the room.

He should do something like this with his living room. He hated what Felicity had done to the room. Luckily, that and the bedroom were the only two rooms she'd redecorated, and she had taken the bedroom furniture with her when she left. It was the only thing she had wanted from him besides money and position. He hadn't given her the position she craved, and there hadn't been much money either when she left. Too bad she hadn't taken the living room furniture.

A myriad of pictures sat on the mantle. Several of an older couple − her parents. Some he guessed were friends or siblings. Several contained shots of Jillian. In one picture she was smiling at the camera with a playful sensuousness that made his breath catch in his chest.

Forcing his attention away, he focused on the painting over the mantel, couple of pintail ducks swimming through reeds set in a cherry-wood frame. The artist did a nice job, picking up the likeness perfectly. Maybe he would see about something like that for his office.

J Taylor, the signature, tucked neatly in the reeds at the corner, caught his attention. Jillian Taylor, he looked around the apartment, did that fit her? It could be a relative, or just coincidence. He eyed the painting.

"Should I put these in a bag?" She stood at the bottom of the stairs in a snug pair of worn jeans and an oversized blue sweater. Comfort clothes. Her arms extended out the bundle of clothes leaving no doubt, she wished never to touch them again.

Quickly he stepped forward taking them. "I'll put them in an evidence bag in the car. Thank you."

"I didn't ask again – were you able to find out anything about Abby, my dog?"

"Sorry. I should've told you before. All I could find out was she had two cuts, and they've taken her to Mountain View Veterinary Clinic. Eliza Jones is the veterinarian there. She handles our police dogs. She's very competent."

The young woman in front of him seemed so vulnerable that it called out to him to do something more. "We can call from the hospital and check on her if you'd like."

"Yes, please." Jillian wrapped her arms around herself.

"Ready?" He motioned to the door.

Jillian hesitated. He guessed she didn't really want to go back out into the dark night. "I'll get my purse since I'll need ID." She waited to move, tension filled the air.

He could see her chin tremble.

"I didn't wash my hands or brush my hair." The words rushed from her lips followed by a half sob.

Mark found himself resisting the urge to step forward and wrap his arms around her. He thought he had won his inner fight when she took another trembling breath. The next thing he realized, his arm went out around her pulling her close. Her head came to rest against his chest, tucked under his chin.

"It's okay now. I'm not going to let anything happen to you." He moved his hand up and down her back. Neither said another word for several moments until Jillian stepped back. He let her go immediately feeling a strange sense of loss.

"I'm ready." She looked up rather shyly before turning to her closet to get her purse.

C3&0

Mark leaned his head back against the wall. He had been in the waiting room nearly two hours. It was past one o'clock. Another night he wasn't home to see Jordan before bedtime. He cursed himself once again. Boys needed their father around them, especially when there wasn't a mother in the home. Mrs. Morris was wonderful. She'd been their housekeeper for nearly three years now, but he knew it wasn't the same for Jordan. He wished Jordan could have it like he did through his youth.

Yeah, sure his dad was always busy and in the public view with his political career, but he always made sure Mark never felt like he was lacking attention. He tried to emulate his father, yet, here it was another night away from his son. Well, no matter what time he finally got to bed, he would make sure he was up to see Jordan before school in the morning.

He looked down the hallway again hoping to see Jillian Taylor coming. If it seemed to be a long night for him, it must feel like an eternity for her. At least he had been able to put some of his time to use.

Through Delaney's market, they had found out the other woman's name was Sandra Cannon. Her parents had been contacted, and he had talked to them for quite a while when they arrived at the hospital, waiting for their daughter to come out of surgery. So far, the prospects were looking good. She was expected to survive though she might be in critical condition for some time.

He had also been able to reach Dr. Jones and find out that Jillian's dog had been stitched up and was going to recover fully. Eliza told him it would be a couple of days until the dog could go home and there wasn't much use coming tonight since the dog was sedated. Now, all Mark had to do was tell Jillian.

He closed his eyes, picturing the woman. The image formed in his mind with surprising clarity. Medium height, honey blonde hair with sun-lightened streaks that he thought were natural. Large blue eyes. Fresh, clean, appealing, so appealing he wanted to gather her in his arms, to protect her from all the mad cruelties of the world. He shuddered at the thought of how well she had fit in his arms back at her apartment.

"Chief Richards." Her voice trickled through him as if he had conjured her up in his mind.

Forcing back the thoughts of her, he opened his eyes, pulling himself upright away from the wall. She looked a little more tired, and now her hair all hung free, brushed into soft touchable wisps around her freshly washed face. The bruise on her cheek stood out a little more pronounced, attesting to the rough night she'd had, but she looked appealing with her blue eyes shadowed in drowsiness, calling for her to be cuddled and held tight.

"They said I can leave." Her voice also was stronger now.

"Are you all right?" He stepped toward her, extending his arm to direct her to the exit.

"The doctor said I'm fine."

He was tempted to ask again how she felt and not what the doctor said but held it in as she continued.

"The officer took my statement, sh … she said it would be typed up and that I could go to the police station tomorrow and sign it. I guess that's normal procedure."

"Yes. If you think of anything more, you can add it at any later time." He closed his hand on her elbow as the doors slid open to the darkness of the night.

⋐⋑⋓⋒

Jillian forced herself to take a deep breath wondering if nighttime would ever feel the same again. A spicy musk smell invaded her senses, warm and appealing. All of her senses must be going haywire tonight.

She shifted to catch a glance of the man beside her in the glow of the dashboard. No, not haywire, Police Chief Richards was an appealing man. She could still feel the tingling awareness of where his fingers had closed on her elbow, and now even after everything that had happened tonight, she felt safe.

Strangely enough, that was how she felt from the first time he had turned to her, and she was caught in those hazel eyes. Security – was that what everyone felt when he looked at them? No wonder he was the police chief. He didn't seem old. In fact, he seemed a lot younger then she would have guessed for the position, maybe mid-thirties.

Shifting again, she turned to get a better look at him. The faint green glow from the speedometer made his face appear harsher, emphasizing his high cheekbones and sharp distinctive nose. A lock of sandy hair curled over his forehead creating a longing within her to touch and trace it with her finger. Shocked at the thought, Jillian looked out the window.

To the side of her, Chief Richards broke the silence. "Is there somewhere else you would like me to take you?"

"All I want is to see how Abby is."

"I called from the hospital. Dr. Jones said your dog will be just fine. Fortunately, none of the wounds were as serious as they appeared to be, but she is sedated and won't wake up until at least morning. Dr. Jones suggested that you wait 'til then to come visit."

"Oh." Jillian couldn't keep in her disappointment.

"I'm sorry." He seemed hesitant to continue. "She also said it would be a couple days before she'd advise taking her home."

"She is all right, isn't she?" Jillian again couldn't keep the tremor from her voice.

"She'll be fine. I promise you, Eliza Jones is very good. But it took fifty-six stitches to sew Abby up. There was one cut on her shoulder and another on the side of her neck."

The shudder came from deep within. Jillian wrapped her arms around her body in attempt to keep from breaking apart. It all seemed so unreal. Tears threatened. "She's just a puppy."

A sob snuck out. She wanted the night to end. She wanted Abby.

⋅⋅⋅

Mark kept his eyes focused into the foggy night lit by the headlights, feeling that if he even glanced at the woman sitting next to him, he'd give in to his urges and pull her into his arms, and never let her go. He clenched his hands on the steering wheel. He was getting too old for these late nighters.

He was a police officer. The Police Chief. She was a victim and a witness. He needed to keep that foremost in his mind. He'd never had a problem doing that before.

It didn't make sense. At thirty-six, he was too old for the fresh-faced young woman sitting next to him. Maybe that was the attraction – fresh, and innocent. Maybe he hadn't been around that type of female for so long that he couldn't deal rationally with it. He felt a most unreasonable compulsiveness toward her.

He wasn't sure how long they'd driven in silence before her voice again trembled through the air.

"Did … did they find him?"

Every muscle in his body tightened to the point that the tension filled the car. "No." It was a low growl, "but we will." It was more a promise to himself than it was to her.

Inside the car it remained silent until they pulled into her condominium.

"Are you sure there's no place that you'd rather I take you for the night?" He shifted into park.

"No, I'd just like to go in, take a hot shower and go to bed."

"We'll have cars in the neighborhood all night," Mark said to give her some comfort.

"Thank you."

Mark heard the catch in her voice and got out before he could give into the desire to take her into his arms to comfort her. What Jillian Taylor needed was for them to catch this monster. That firmly in his mind, he walked her to her door and left after making sure all was secure.

It was only a short trip to his house. The light in the hall welcomed him to the otherwise dark and silent house. All was peaceful here not much more than a mile from the crime that wreaked havoc on his night's sleep.

He wondered if Jillian would sleep that night. He doubted it. Twice he almost found himself volunteering to stay with her. Luckily, his reasonable side had stopped him, reminding him about not getting personally involved with a case. After all, she was a victim. The last thing she needed to deal with was an amorous police chief.

He opened the fridge, pulled out his dinner, and slid it into the microwave. At the bell, he took it out only to push the food around the plate while thinking over everything that had happened tonight.

At least now, they had some evidence to work with. They would get this guy. But would it be before someone else died? He didn't want to think of the possibility. Shoving a bite of food in his mouth, he found it cold again.

He gave up and put it back in the fridge. He'd have to be up in a few hours to see Jordan off to school. It was a practice he had always tried to maintain no matter what the situation. He wanted his son to know that he was the most important thing in his life.

Slowly he walked up the stairs, carrying his shoes not to make extra noise. He paused at Jordan's door and looked in at the sleeping boy, his son. Jordan was the only good to come out of his four-year marriage. He had a lot of regrets about Felicity, but none about his son. There was no question Jordan was his son. They were the same in looks and in actions.

Pride swelled within him. Turning away, he went to his room. After shucking his clothes, he stretched out on his bed. Unimpeded, his thoughts again went to Jillian Taylor.

ఴఴ

The water didn't seem to be hot enough to wash the terrors of the night away. Shuddering at the feeling of the darkness peering in through the fan window high on the wall, Jillian slammed off the water. She pulled the large, soft towel around her flushed body. She wouldn't be scared. This was her house. She was safe here, and she wasn't going to let anything convince her otherwise.

She was strong, strong enough to cut off the urge to plead with Chief Richards to stay with her awhile. She was safe. She repeated the phrase in her mind again. The windows and doors were locked. The alarm was on. Chief Richards had gone through the whole condo making sure it was clear before he left, but as soon as she watched him pull away, she wished she could bring him back. For some reason, safety and warmth had become synonymous with him.

She pulled on another pair of old, warm sweats, curled up on the bed, and dragged the covers up around her. Willing herself to sleep was no good. Each noise, real or imaginary, had her bolting upright again. She wished Abby was there or maybe a police chief with a strong chin and broad shoulders.

ఴఴ

The shadow closed in on her. Jillian ran harder. She had to find Abby. She could hear her whining. Jillian called for her, panicking as trees lashed out at her, then the branches changed into knives swiping out.

Jillian screamed.

Abby's whine. She was close. She could find her.

Jillian burst through the mist and froze at the sight of

the castle towering over her. It was no shimmering, fairy tale castle with sparkling towers and bright colored banners. It was dark, ominous with heavy turrets and deep shadows.

A whine drew her forward against her will. "Abby." Jillian stepped on the drawbridge and almost pulled back as something moved in the murky goo of the moat.

Terror threatened to crush her, but she kept going on. The bars of the gate slithered under her hand. Jillian swallowed and pushed it open, forcing herself on. "Abby." She turned toward the sound of barking. The scream ripped from her throat as she looked at the beast covered in darkness.

"Scream for me, Beauty. Love me, Beauty."

"No!" Jillian sprang up in bed. Sweat drenched her body. Her heart fought for each beat. The familiarity of her room seeped in, but the terror refused to fade. Jillian pulled her legs to her chest, wrapped her arms around them and dropped her head down, trying to catch her breath among tears.

When she managed to get herself in control enough to move, she looked at the clock. The digital number read five-twelve. A glance at the darkness outside her balcony glass doors confirmed the truthfulness of the time. Taking a deep breath, she tried to push her fear away as her heart rate slid closer to normal.

Jillian looked at the window again. It wasn't totally dark because of the condo's lights along the walkways, but unfortunately, she couldn't make the sun rise sooner. Still, she could refuse to let the night beat her.

Knowing there was no going back to sleep, she pushed aside the blanket. She went to the bathroom, pulled out a clean towel and turned on the shower that she had only left a couple hours earlier. This time the shower was a little more successful in washing away the night's terror.

Cuddled in the thick robe that had been a present to

herself on her last birthday, she wandered around unable to settle down. After the third trip up and down the stairs, Jillian decided she'd had enough and headed for her closet. Taking out what she labeled her power suit, she dressed. A few minutes later, she had her hair twisted up in a French knot and headed for her car.

Once in the seat, she hit the button on the garage door opener and started the car. The door hardly cleared the car before she backed out. The faint morning glow started to light the streets, but the shadows were still too deep, pulling a shudder from her, but she pressed on.

With no traffic to slow her down, it took only a couple minutes to reach her design studio, Taylored Interiors. The sight of it gave her a jolt of pleasure even the ugliness of the night couldn't dim. She had worked so hard the last couple years, given up a lot on a personal and social life, but it had paid off. Her client base was getting stronger every day. She had all the work she could handle. Now was a perfect time to spend a couple of extra uninterrupted hours.

At the door, she felt a moment's hesitation until she hit the light switch. Light flooded the studio bringing it alive with color. This was her work space. Here she ruled. The wave of confidence rushed over her wiping away any doubt. Clicking the lock behind her was normal practice when she was there alone after hours.

CR80

"Jillian."

Jillian jumped. A whole row of markers clattered to the floor. Her shriek ended in more of a squeak as she spun to face Nan. Jillian dropped her head to her hand propped on the table as the other hand came to her chest.

"Sorry, I didn't realize you didn't hear me unlock the doors."

"I guess … I got caught up."

"Submerged might be a better word." Then the woman

who was her assistant really looked at her. Jillian feared for a moment that Nan would see the bruises under the layer of makeup, but the woman shifted her attention to her desk and the surrounds. "What's all this? How long you been here?" She motioned to her jacket on the back of the chair and the design boards strung along the wall and stacked on her desk.

"A while, I couldn't sleep so decided it was better to work through it." Jillian shrugged.

"Work being the optimum word. What's this one?" Nan grimaced, looking at a board next to the waste basket. "Definitely not your usual quality."

Jillian met the grimace with one of her own. "It took me a minute to get into it."

"I'd say. Want to tell me what's wrong?"

"It's nothing."

"This is me, Sweet Pea. Want to try again?"

"I'm glad you don't call me that around the clients."

Nan had a handful of flower nick names she called her. The woman treated her more like a daughter than an employer, but that was how their relationship worked and it worked great.

A year ago, Jillian was looking for help around the studio, figuring she'd find a college student. She ended up with a fifty-year-old woman who had her family all raised and moved away and needed something productive to do with her time. The combination was perfect. Nan had great taste, was extremely efficient, and watched after Jillian like a mother hen.

Nan remained silent, staring down at her, Jillian fidgeted in her chair. "It doesn't matter."

Nan's eyebrow arched. "Now, if you were dating someone, I'd say you broke up last night. But, since you hardly take time to go out, and the only males you have penciled in your life right now are ten and eleven years old and wear shin guards, I'm not buying that, so give. What's happened since yesterday? You didn't lose the Van Buren account? No, that's what you're working on, and it wouldn't do this to you."

"Do what?"

"Upset you so. There's a … shadowed quality about you today."

"That bad?"

"No, not that bad, but you forget, I know you."

Jillian sighed. There was going to be no getting around it. Besides, it would probably be best to talk it out, and there was no one better to talk to than Nan. "Remember a month ago about the young woman who was murdered? It made the news for several days because it was similar to another."

"Yes." Trepidation tightened Nan's voice. "Jillian, what happened, Poppy?"

"Last night, when Abby and I were running, she broke away. I raced after her. We … there was … he was going to kill her. Abby stopped him. She saved her. Then he tried to kill me."

"Jillian!" Nan wrapped her arms around her.

The tears she'd been holding back broke free to run down her cheeks as she soaked in the comfort.

After a moment she pulled back. "I'm okay. Abby saved me, too. But he cut her. Then the police got there. She's at the vet's. I haven't been able to see her yet." She wiped her eyes and looked at the clock. "The vet should be open by now, don't you think?"

"Yes, of course. Do you have the number? I'll check."

Jillian shook her head. "Chief Richards said it was Mountain View."

"All right, you go clean up. I'll call and change your morning appointments to give you some time."

Jillian nodded her thanks. She felt better again. "I also have to go to the police station and sign a statement."

"We'll figure that in, too."

Ψ

Jillian spent an hour with Abby, who just wanted to cuddle up in her lap. It was a habit she'd had been trying to break her of, but at that moment Jillian didn't mind it or the yellow hairs on her black skirt. She was just happy to see Abby doing so well. Even the fact that she couldn't bring her home until the next day, and there would be no runs for a while didn't dull her pleasure.

Next, she stopped at the hospital to check on Sandra but found they wouldn't release any information since she wasn't a relative. As she turned to leave, an older man approached her.

"Excuse me. I heard you asking about my daughter. You said you were at the park last night?"

"Yes. I was jogging with my dog."

"You're the one who saved her."

"Actually, it was my dog that did. How's Sandra?"

"I was just headed to the cafeteria. Would you join me?"

She nodded, letting him lead her away from the desk.

"She survived the night," Sandra's father said wearily. "The doctors are now hopeful, but they cautioned us it will be sometime before we know anything for sure. She would not have had that chance if not for you and your dog."

"We just happened to be there at the right time." Jillian suppressed a shudder. Until then she'd been feeling like it was bad luck being there. Now, talking with Sandra's father it gave her a whole new perspective. Something good had come out of it. Sandra was alive.

Her father went on to thank her again. Her mind clung to the positive as they exchanged numbers and promises to keep in touch.

Jillian felt better as she headed to the police station. On the stone steps leading into the building, a blast of apprehension hit her, freezing her in place as her heart raced. She felt faint. She didn't want to think of the attack, definitely didn't want to read it.

Her nails dug into her palms as she forced her foot to the next step. She could do this. It was nothing. She just had to look over the report then sign it. No big deal, she tried to convince herself. Her stomach clenched, and she thought she'd be sick.

She didn't want to think, didn't want to remember The Beast and the fear. Unwanted, the image formed in her mind, dark, shadowy and menacing. She staggered back a step.

When had she dubbed him 'The Beast' in her mind? In her dream, when she heard him call her Beauty. Well, there was no love for this Beast. He killed, and he hurt Abby. She forced the image away, replacing it with Abby – her sweet, loving puppy. Abby saved Sandra, and Abby saved her. The Beast would have killed Sandra. And, he would kill again if he wasn't stopped. She would do anything to stop him.

Chapter Four

Pulling her confidence tight around her, Jillian started back up the steps, plastering on the smile she saved for difficult clients or challenging contractors. She was greeted inside the door by two police officers standing beside a metal detector.

"May I help you, ma'am?" the officer on her right asked. He was large, intimidating, with a buzz cut so short his skin glistened beneath it.

"I …" She took a deep breath, telling herself again that she could do this. "I was told to come and sign a statement."

"All right." He gentled his countenance with a smile. "Just put your purse, keys, and cell phone in one of the bins and step through, then you head to the desk over there, and the sergeant will instruct you from there."

"Thank you."

She took in the whole floor. The designer in her observed the area from the good quality, gray commercial carpet to the sand colored walls. There were several paintings, not expensive by any means, but they were pleasant. She felt a touch more comfortable. The cells and holding rooms must be somewhere else in the building. She realized that it made sense not to bring anyone dangerous in the same entrance as the visitors came in. Still, it looked a whole lot different from the police station she had visited on a field trip in elementary school.

The officer at the desk turned his attention to her. He seemed young. He kicked up his smile as he looked her over. "May I help you?"

"Yes. I was to come in and sign a statement." She managed to say without her voice trembling.

"Who was the officer in charge of your case?"

"I … I don't know. There were so many there."

He looked surprised. "Okay, no problem. Can you tell me one of their names or what the case was concerning so I can look it up?"

"Chief Richards was there, and there was an Edwards." Jillian stopped as the officer's face grew very serious.

"The park last night?"

She nodded, feeling her throat tighten.

"You're the witness?"

She figured his expression was as much awe as disbelief. "I was jogging with my dog."

He nodded. "Let me see who's handling it and who is here."

He picked up the phone and punched an extension. After a minute, she heard him ask, "Well, who's here covering? All right." He hung up the phone and looked to her. "I'm sorry. All the leads on the case are gone at the moment or tied up. If you'll give me a second I'll check who's on rotation and see if they can pull the statement." He made another call then turned to her. "If you'll just take the elevator to the third floor Detective Crocker will meet you."

"Thank you."

A second later, Jillian stepped out onto a floor buzzing with activity. Men and women sat at desks, some on the phone, others talking, and typing.

"I'm Detective Crocker. I wasn't given your name."

Jillian pulled back, startled at the officer's gruff manner. He was medium height, slightly stocky, not bad looking. In fact, he might have been handsome if he'd been clean shaven and didn't look so slothful. "Taylor, Jillian Taylor."

"Sit at the second desk over there, I'll get the paperwork." The man walked away leaving her standing there.

Jillian shrugged and crossed the room, receiving several curious looks. The detective returned, reading from the folder in his hands and shaking his head. He sat down across the desk and glared at her. "When will you women ever learn?"

"Excuse me?"

"You go out, put yourselves in a position you should never be in, then cry when something happens."

Jillian was so surprised at the venom in his voice she couldn't answer.

"Here read this." He shoved the file at her.

Jillian opened the file. A minute later, she found herself fighting to read each word. Even down in clinical clarity, they tore at her, bringing all that happened to harsh focus.

"Is there anything you want to add or change?" The words bit at the already shaky hold on her control.

"No, no, it's complete." She tried to calm her anxiety. "I'm sorry." She wiped at a tear that threatened to break free.

The man shook his head in undisguised disgust. "What did you expect? Next time you decide to put yourself in a dangerous position, try growing a brain and don't."

Jillian felt the fire in her flare. "You make this sound like it was my fault. Do you think it was Sandra's too? After all, she was walking home from work."

"She should never have been walking alone so late, nor

should you. You women ought to know that, or you should expect something to happen."

"You can't believe that a victim deserves what they get and be a police officer. It's just … there's no way. Sandra's a nice girl. She's hardworking and friendly. She does not deserve to be lying in the hospital. She didn't do anything to justify this guy trying to kill her."

"You don't know that."

"Oh yes, I do. I saw this man. He's sick. A psycho. He doesn't care who he kills or hurts. He's just going to continue."

"And you just gave him an excuse. Because he's sick! See that's it. It's always 'I was sick. I couldn't help myself. I came from a poor background. Neglected. Drugs made me do it.' It's all the same excuse, and they walk out free and clear. So, if you don't want it happening to you, then you shouldn't go out alone in places like dark alleys, parks, alone in parking lots, or deserted streets. If you do, you deserve what you get."

Jillian was furious. She wanted to shake some sense into the man. She couldn't believe he thought that way, but it was there plainly on his face that he did. She grabbed the pen lying on his desk and scrawled her name on the signature line.

"Here." She shoved the folder at him. "Good day, Detective." She bit back the retort that wanted to explode out. Placing the pen on the desk instead of throwing it at him, she was on her feet heading out.

The crude comments from a punk handcuffed to a chair didn't penetrate her anger as she stormed across the room, her heels clicking on the tile. She didn't wait for the elevator. Pushing open the stairway door, the only thing going through her mind was she had to get out of there. She took the steps at a reckless pace. Jillian was out the door and halfway down the block before she realized she was going the wrong way. Her car was parked the opposite direction.

Tears escaped. Deflated, she leaned back against the building, feeling drained, thinking it all had to be a nightmare. It couldn't be true, it just couldn't. The denial didn't keep the ghastly images from flipping through her mind. She shuddered, pushed away from the wall, and focused on her surroundings. She was not going to let nightmares, fear, or a soured, dim-witted, judgmental – correction – just mental police officer break her.

By the time she got back to the studio, she had herself under control again, but the newspaper Nan showed her didn't help. On the front page was a blurry, but still discernible, picture of her being sheltered by the police chief. Well, so much for sheltering. She'd go with Detective Crocker's advice and take care of herself. She didn't need any handsome police chief looking after her. A pang zipped through her heart as the thought went through her head.

"Lousy picture quality. They need a better photographer." Sarcasm slid out.

"You okay, Buttercup?"

The endearment once more deflated her like nothing else could have. Jillian poured it all out to the older woman.

"Well, that obnoxious jerk. I can't believe they have someone like that dealing with people. What are they thinking?" Nan steamed.

"I don't know, but I've done my duty. I never want to see a policeman ever again."

The woman looked like she was going to say something back then made a shooing motion. "You go sit in the alcove and relax, and I'll bring you a nice soothing cup of tea. There's almost an hour before Mrs. Ostermiller gets here. I already have her stuff all laid out."

☙❧

Mark spied her the moment he walked into Taylored Interiors. Jillian Taylor was the picture of polish and poise.

How could a woman look so perfect after almost being killed by a psychotic, serial killer only eighteen hours earlier?

His irritation rose. This was the woman he'd been worried about. The woman the night before who'd looked soft and sweet. The one who attracted him like he hadn't been in a long, long time.

He made a mental shake of his head. Hadn't he learned his lesson from his wife not to get caught up with a polished, professional woman who didn't deal with the everyday normalness of his life? Not that he considered Jillian Taylor for himself. She was just a witness in a case – a witness who had been put in potential danger.

He smacked the newspaper against his leg. He'd like to get his hands on a certain reporter right now. He had some frustration to vent. Unable to do that, he approached Jillian Taylor.

He caught the action as she glanced in his direction then away, dismissing him. He felt his irritation double. He continued forward sparing only a fleeting glance at the alcoves that held tastefully displays of fabrics, carpets, and materials in an array of textures. His ex-wife would have been right in her element, lapping it all up.

Putting it out of his mind, he focused on Jillian Taylor. Before he could reach her, he was cut off by an attractive brunette in her mid-fifties.

"May I help you?" she asked moving in front of him as he started to sidestep her.

"I need to talk to Miss Taylor."

"She's with a client at the moment. She shouldn't be long if you'd like to have a seat over here. I'll get you some refreshments while you wait." The whole thing was said extremely pleasantly but he had no doubt the woman was like a rhino protecting its young. For all her aged sweetness, he'd bet she had a hide as tough as steel and a temper that could be vicious when riled.

He debated a moment, then nodded and followed the woman to a sitting area in the back of another alcove.

"Juice or tea?"

"Water, please."

The woman nodded and walked off, glancing back at him. Mark ignored her, focusing on the other voices. It wasn't hard to pick up Jillian Taylor's. The tone was still as soft as the night before, but it sounded more confident.

"I'll get those drawings done right away so you can choose the look. I'll also double check the availability, but I should be able to get them scheduled with the other installation the first of next week."

"That would be wonderful, dear. You're such a gem. Your ideas have been just perfect. It's like you can read my mind about what I want." The woman continued to chat.

Mark glanced at his watch. Five minutes passed, then ten, and the woman still showed no sign of leaving. Reaching the end of his patience, he placed both hands on the arms of the chair and pushed up just as the woman stood.

"Gracious, look at the time. I'd better hurry home. Henry and I are going to the club tonight. Thank you so much, dear."

"You're welcome, Mrs. Ostermiller. You have a good evening, and I'll be in touch in a few days."

Jillian stood, seeing the woman to the door and giving Mark his first view of her nylon clad legs. Trim ankles and nice shaped calves were set off by a pair of three inch heels and trim cut black skirt. The light-blue of the silk shirt she wore set her eyes to fire, or maybe it was the sparks she shot at him when she finally turned to him that made him think of fire.

"Chief." She nodded her head, but her actions were rigid and non-welcoming.

Mark's first instinct was to bite back, but his diplomacy held out. "Miss Taylor." He kept his greeting formal. "I've been trying to reach you all day."

"I'm sorry." Her tone belied the apology. "I've been busy with appointments, and since I already stopped at the station earlier to go over my statement, I saw no further need."

"I'm afraid I missed you at the station, and I assure you there is a great need to talk with you."

"I can't imagine why."

She played verbal cat and mouse very well he decided, but it was time to close the trap. He held up the newspaper, displaying the fuzzy picture of her, taken just as he shifted to shield her.

"I've seen the picture." She glanced at it and quickly away. "I cannot say I'm pleased."

"Nor I. I would like to discuss some precautions with you."

"Precautions?" She turned back, startled, and in that instant he saw the woman from the night before who had ignited his protective instincts, but she was gone as quickly as she appeared. Back was the firm, polished businesswoman. "What do you mean?"

"First, I would like to discuss some security."

"Actually, I don't have time right now."

"Miss Taylor, I must insist. This is your life we're talking about."

"Don't worry about it. I was already informed today that if a woman was stabbed by some psycho, it's her own fault. She shouldn't be on her own. So there's no need to repeat the lecture. I assure you it was quite clear the first time." Anger poured off her.

"I'm afraid I've missed something here. Maybe we could try this again if you'd give me a minute."

She was already shaking her head. "I really must go."

His aggravation spiked and he didn't try to temper it. "I'm sure your client can wait ten minutes."

"It's not a client." She cut him off.

"Then your date," he snapped back.

"It's not a date." She glanced at her watch. "I have to go."

"I need to discuss limiting who you see. Especially going out alone."

"I assure you I'll be cautious. I'm not a fool, but if you think I'm going to limit my business, it's not going to happen. I'm just beginning to build my reputation. I can't endanger that now. Besides, the picture isn't that good, and they don't have my name. He can't know who I am. Also, I do plan on avoiding the park for a while. Now, if you'll excuse me."

She strode away, stopping long enough to grab her purse. "Nan, I'm leaving now. See you in the morning." She called loud enough to carry to the back where the other woman had disappeared.

"Be careful." Nan appeared from another alcove.

"I will. Why don't you lock up now? Bye." She turned back, pausing as Mark blocked her way. "Chief Richards?"

Mark got the feeling she was going to brush by him then she paused. "Thank you for coming and for your concern, but I assure you I'll be fine on my own. But, if I do have a problem, I'll let you know."

Mark nodded, having to accept that. Reaching into his breast pocket, he pulled out a card. "This has the number where I can always be reached." He handed it to her. "Anytime."

Jillian raised an eyebrow, nodding again as she turned from him, and he followed her out to a four-year-old, white compact. It was a nice, sensible car that got good gas mileage and top safety records. He approved of her choice in cars. Still, a frown clouded his features. He didn't like her refusal to listen to him.

⊂ℜ≈

Mark was back to steaming by the time he entered his office. He should've known she was too good to be true.

What was he thinking last night? That was why you shouldn't get personally involved. Not that he was personally involved, but okay, he was interested. Was, being the definitive word.

She seemed so ... sweet, innocent. Something about her drew him, but it was all a cheap facade that she donned like a mask to get help and attention. Luckily, the illusion crumbled before he made a major mistake, like actually asking her out.

He crumpled the paper in his hand and threw it across the room. She was just like his ex-wife, driven by image and power. What flaw was it in him that attracted him to that kind of women? Okay, so yes, he was attracted. She was beautiful. How could he miss that she was just an illusion with nothing solid and warm about her? You'd think that as many years as he'd been a police officer, he'd be better at seeing through lies.

He starred out the window at nothing.

"Chief."

His name, said behind him, pulled him back from his reverie. "Yeah." He turned to Andrew Hamilton standing in the doorway.

"We may have a problem."

"What is it?" he asked while thinking. "Like I don't have several problems already."

"It seems that while you, Edward, and I were out of the station today our witness came in to sign her statement. They turned her over to Crocker."

"He's not on the case."

"Yeah, well, we were out. Everyone else was busy. Anyway, Joey said she looked pretty upset when she left."

Mark bit back a curse. "Why didn't he take her?"

"He was tied up with the Simmons case. He'd just brought in the suspect, but he noticed our witness come in. You know − beautiful, kind of nervous, frightened. Hey, his words not mine." Andrew lifted his hands, obviously reading that he was about to explode. "Anyway, he wanted to give us heads up that she looked more like a hostile witness when she stormed out."

"Stormed out?"

Andrew nodded. "That's a quote."

"What else?" He saw the detective shift and grimace.

"That she looked like she was flaming and about to chew nails. He said she was spectacular."

Mark bit back another curse which was something he seldom had to do. He had never developed a habit of swearing, but from the time Jordan was born, he was extra careful. "Crocker isn't to be handling anyone. He's on desk jobs – busy work."

"We have someone new on the desk who didn't know, and Crocker's name was up on rotation."

"All right, thanks. I'll take care of it."

"Uh, Chief, what are you going to do?"

"Something that I should've done a couple months ago." He sighed, "Put him on mandatory leave until he completes psychiatric counseling and can come to grips with his girlfriend's death. I know he said he just needs time to work it out, and Wilcox was trying to give it to him. But, he's not getting better, and this isn't the first problem we've had." Mark sighed again. "It's getting worse."

Mark couldn't help but wonder if some of Miss Taylor's coolness was anger at his department, or if he was just looking for excuses. "I think I'm going to have to offer a departmental apology to our witness. Hostile is a fitting description of what she was when I visited her."

He shoved his fingers back through his hair. "But first, get me that reporter on the phone and while you're at it, I want his editor, too. I want to know what they were thinking when they posted our witness's picture on the front page. I'm not happy at all about them putting her life in danger. This is nothing about freedom of the press or the people have a right to know. It's plain stupidity."

"That ought to be a good way to work off some anger. I'll get them on the line now." The man left with a cocky grin.

◌◌

Jillian deflected the soccer ball, sending it to midfield then blew her whistle ending the scrimmage. "All right guys, everyone over," she called to the team of ten and eleven year old boys and waited while they all ran up.

"Good practice. Now, I don't want you to worry about the game tomorrow. It's everyone's first game. I expect to see a lot of mistakes, but I want to see you working together and trying to incorporate some of the things we've practiced in the drills. Cover your positions. Pass. No ball hogs. Soccer can't be won by one person. And I really don't want to see anyone get after anyone else for a mistake. We stay positive, and mainly, we have a good time. What's our rule?" she yelled out at the end.

"Play hard, play fair and have fun!" they yelled back.

"Right! It looks like rides are here. See you in the morning. Don't forget to grab your ball and water bottles."

The boys chattered excitedly as they headed for the cars.

"Sam, can you grab the cones for me?" she asked.

"Sure, Jillian," her neighbor boy returned as she reached for the ball bag.

"Can I help?" Jordan volunteered.

Glancing over first to see that no one appeared to be waiting for him, she answered, "Sure." Jillian watched a second as the boys, who were becoming friends, raced off and smiled. It was nice to see Sam making friends.

He was a slim, black-haired, dark complexioned boy with soulful eyes who stole your heart. He and his mother had moved a couple doors down from her three months earlier. They had become fast friends just as these boys were becoming.

Jordan could hardly be more opposite. He was quite

44

tall for his age. His fairer skin was well tanned. He had sandy blond hair with sun-bleached streaks that were almost white. His eyes were an intriguing combination of gray-green. A good looking boy. She smiled. Both boys would have their share of girls falling for them when they got older. The little heartbreakers had no idea yet.

Turning back, she reached for another ball when a shiver ran through her. Jillian froze, studying the area, seeing nothing. She gave herself a mental shake and reached again for her ball as the boys ran up to drop the cones in the equipment bag.

She jumped when a horn honked.

"Oh, that's Mrs. Morris. I've got to go. See ya, Sam. Bye, Jillian." Jordan rushed off.

"Bye. Ready to go?" Jillian turned to Sam.

"Yeah, Mom should be home soon."

With one more nervous glance back at the soccer field, Jillian, suppressed another shiver and she turned to Sam. "Ready?" She grabbed the bag of balls and cones while Sam took the smaller one.

"That was fun," he said as he fell into step with her.

"Did I do okay then?" Jillian looked over at the boy.

"You're great. At first, the guys were groaning about having a girl coach, but they think you're awesome now. You know a lot more than Thomas's dad did."

"Well, that's good to know. I think they're awesome, too."

"Do you think we'll win tomorrow?"

She smiled, of course that would be on his mind. "I don't know. It's our first game; this was only our second practice, but you guys worked really hard, so I don't know why not."

"Hi, Jillian."

Jillian yelped and dropped the bag. "Oh, Toby," she gasped, placing her hand over her heart, trying to catch her breath. "You scared me."

"I'm sorry, Jillian. I just wanted to say hi." The large, well-built man scuffed his foot along the ground like a chastened child, which was more like what Toby was.

"Hi, Toby." Jillian forced a smile and greeted the man. She liked Toby. He worked at the same grocery store as Sandra. A spike of fear ran through her at the thought of the night before.

"I didn't know you played soccer." Toby's statement brought her back to the present.

Sam answered before she could. "She's our coach. She's great."

"You're a coach? Can I be on your team? I love to play soccer. I can kick the ball real hard." This time he shifted back and forth hopefully.

"I'm sorry, Toby, you can't be on the team if you're over twelve." Mentally, she knew that was about where Toby was, but physically, he was twenty-two, about six feet two inches and easily twice any of the boys' weight. At the moment, he looked so downhearted, she couldn't keep back the next words. "But, I'll tell you what, if you see us practicing again, you can come over and play if you promise to listen to me and do what I say. You can be my helper, okay?"

"Oh, wow. I can do it. I'll listen and do just what you say." The smile radiated from him. "Can I carry your bag?"

She handed it over though they weren't far from the car. He lifted the big, awkward bag with ease.

"Do you need a ride home, Toby?" she asked as he lifted the bag into her trunk.

"No, thanks, I have my car." He pointed to a beat up hatchback with oxidizing red paint and a collection of things hanging from the rear view mirror.

"All right. Well, Sam, we'd better get you back to your mom. She'll be wondering where you are. See you later, Toby."

As she pulled away, Jillian glanced in the rearview

mirror to see Toby staring after them. She knew he had a crush on her. She just didn't know how to discourage it without hurting him. He really was nice, kind of like a big puppy. She felt a wave of sadness.

He was a good looking man, in fact, very handsome with light brown hair that was slightly shaggy and soulful brown eyes. The only thing that marred his looks was a scar that ran from the top of his cheekbone back into his hair on his right side; leftover evidence of the final beating his father had given him. A beating his body recovered from, but his mind never would. It was so sad that Toby would always be limited in his abilities and opportunities in life over such a senseless brutal act.

❧

"Hi, Dad, you're home in time for dinner." Jordan greeted Mark as he stepped through the door from the garage.

It felt good to be home after the night and day he'd had. "Hey, it smells great."

"Yeah, Mrs. Morris fixed baked chicken, potatoes, and homemade rolls."

"I'm definitely glad I made it home."

"We even have chocolate cake."

"And if you two wash up, we can eat in about five minutes." Mrs. Morris cut in.

"Won't get any arguments from me," Mark pulled off his tie, turning to his son. "You want to come up with me?"

"Sure." Jordan followed him to the stairs.

"Are you going to tell me about your day? It must've been something good to give Mrs. Morris time to make such a dinner."

"I had soccer practice. It was great. We have a new coach, since Thomas's dad's job changed, and he couldn't coach. It's a girl, but it's okay. She's really good. She's Sam's next-door neighbor. Man, she's good. None of us can take the ball from her on one-on-one. We had to do a lot of drills, then we played a scrimmage. It was a great practice. We have a game tomorrow, can you come?"

"I'm already planning on it. Thought we'd go for pizza or hamburgers after. What do you say?" He threw his dress shirt in the hamper and reached for a T-shirt.

"Awesome." Together they washed their hands.

"Good, let's go eat and then I thought that we'd settle down in the family room to watch the movie that, if I remember right, you were hinting to me to bring home."

"All right!"

Chapter Five

Mark pulled into the parking space and scanned the soccer field. It was a perfect day for the soccer season to start. Clear blue sky and not overly hot. "Do you see any of your team?"

Jordan looked around then pointed. "There's Sam."

"Okay, let's go." The words were hardly out of his mouth before Jordan was out of the car running over to the field.

Mark stopped to pull a lawn chair out of the trunk then followed his son.

"Dad, this is Sam and my coach."

"Hi, Sam." Mark turned to his son's coach and felt like he'd been hit with a bolt of lightning. From the look on Jillian Taylor's face, it wasn't any less of an impact for her. He couldn't believe it. Here she was again. She was breathtaking.

The glorious, long hair was pulled back in a ponytail. Her face appeared free of make-up except to cover the bruises he knew she must have, and a touch of lip gloss. She wore a light-blue T-shirt that brought out the stunning blue of her eyes. The navy shorts showed off her long, tanned legs.

"Chief." The word brought him back, and Mark realized he had been holding his breath as he stared at her.

"Off duty today. It's Mark." He held out a hand. Awareness sparked as she took it, but she didn't release the touch. "Jillian."

"Hey, Dad, you know Jillian?"

She pulled back, and he could swear her cheeks looked flushed. Well, good. It was nice to know he wasn't the only one feeling something here that had nothing to do with fear or aggravation.

"I met her the other day on a case I'm handling." He shifted his gaze. "How are you?"

"Fine, thank you."

"How's Abby? I checked with the vet yesterday, but I didn't ask you."

"She's doing well. I get to pick her up this afternoon."

"You know her dog got hurt." This time it was Sam who spoke up.

"Yes, she has a wonderful dog. I plan on getting her a treat." Mark looked at Sam, and found both boys were watching them.

"Abby is great," Sam agreed.

"Can I meet your dog, Jillian? What kind is it?" Jordan asked.

"She's a yellow Lab. Maybe I'll bring her to practice when she gets better. But she'd be a pest. She'll want to chase the ball and run with you boys. Why don't you go warm up on the side and get the other boys stretching out as they get here?" When the boys moved off, she glanced up at him. "I didn't realize."

"I didn't either. Last night Jordan had practice. Why didn't you say where you were going?" He felt like he was seeing another part of Jillian Taylor, and he wanted to investigate.

She looked over at the game in progress then back at him. "I wasn't really happy with the police at the moment, and then you came on," she paused as if looking for the right word, "strong. It ticked me off."

"I'd like to apologize for that. I'd just dealt with a press conference when I saw the newspaper. I didn't hear what happened at the station until after I got back. Detective Crocker is off the active list. There was a mix-up. He wasn't to be dealing with people, especially women."

"I'd say that's a good idea." She paused. "Something bad happened?"

Mark noticed that the question in her voice seemed to go beyond plain curiosity, so he answered. "His girlfriend was killed. She went to a bad area, late at night, to surprise him. It was pretty brutal. Crocker is having trouble dealing with it. Anyone would, but he was one of the first on the scene. The other officer didn't recognize her and hold him back."

"How awful."

"Yeah, sorry to bring a downer to your day right before a game."

"No, that's okay. At least now I can understand."

"Well, I'm forcing him to get help before he can return to duty. I do want to apologize again that you had such a bad experience."

"I'm not sure it would've been a good experience anyway." She shuddered.

"Hey, I'm sorry to bring it up." He felt like an idiot. He needed to go back to How to Talk to Women 101. He reached and caught her hand. The instant his fingers touched hers it didn't matter. The connection was back, or maybe it was never broken. She hadn't been far from his thoughts from the moment he'd seen her wrapped in the slate gray blanket from a cruiser. Just as it had been in the middle of that dark, misty night, he wanted to take her in his arms.

"Hey coach!" The call penetrated his mind, and he realized where they were.

"Oh." Jillian pulled back as if she, too, was coming back to reality. "I have to … I'd better–" She looked flustered as she turned from him to her team. "Okay, listen up."

The boys clustered around her, and she beamed with pleasure as she went over their positions with them. They moved onto the field as soon as the other game finished. Mark unfolded his lawn chair but didn't sit in it, too occupied with watching Jordan and his coach.

With the boys running through a drill, Jillian jogged over to meet the other coach and the referee. She was beautiful to watch, a natural athlete with an easy grace. He realized he was seeing a big part of Jillian Taylor. He liked this part.

"Pretty lady. Lucky boys."

There was no mistaking the voice. Mark scowled as he turned. "What are you doing here, Clark?" He didn't try to disguise his displeasure at seeing the reporter.

"Hey, I apologized for the photo. Like I said, I never thought it would be a problem, didn't think that it would be that big a secret, and I'm sad to say it wasn't a very good photo."

"You have a brain, at least you say you do. You should've known."

"Now, is that any way for a police chief to talk to the press?"

Mark just glared and repeated his earlier question. "What are you doing here?"

"Boss wants a story on the new soccer season starting."

"You don't do human interest."

"Sure I do. I'm a man of many talents and we're shorthanded. So what are you doing here?"

"My son is playing."

"Really, which one is yours?"

"Over there." He nodded to the boys taking shots on

goal.

"Ah yes, I can see. He looks like you." Then he let out a low whistle and raised the camera he had hanging around his neck. "Those are some nice legs. Don't see many kids' coaches that look like that."

He was about to snap the picture when Mark grabbed the camera and pulled it down.

"Hey, what do you think you're doing?" The reporter turned belligerent. "You going for police brutality?"

"No, I just don't want you taking that picture. Why don't you take a picture of the other team?" Mark suggested smoothly.

"The other team doesn't have a coach that looks like that. She can't have a child old enough to play. Hey, I know her. Isn't that your witness? She's even pretty in the daylight, a real beauty. So, how'd she end up here? And since when does the police chief do witness protection?"

"Purely coincidence. She was here when I got here."

"What's she doing here when she doesn't have any children?"

"How do you know she doesn't have children?"

"I have my ways. So why's she here?"

"Hey, you have your ways." Mark shot back, watching Jillian still talking to the older man in a ref uniform. After a minute, they shook hands. She called the boys to the center of the field to line up for inspection before they headed for the side.

☙❧

Jillian froze when she saw the reporter standing with Mark Richards. Fear shot through her as did flashes of the night she longed to forget.

"Jillian, Jillian, Miss Taylor." Several of the boys called her attention.

"Yes." She jerked, turning to them. "Grab a quick drink. You know your positions. Let's circle up first, ready."

Together the boys yelled their cheer. "Play hard, play fair, and have fun." Their hands came up in the air as they finished, then they did as she instructed. She waited a moment before she continued toward the men and her duffle bag.

"This should make a good story after all." The reporter stepped forward. "Miss Taylor, I'm Nigel Clark from the newspaper," Clark greeted. "I'm here doing an article on youth soccer and the volunteers. You don't look old enough to have a child out there. Is it a brother or nephew you're coaching?"

Jillian glanced toward Mark before answering. "Just a neighbor, but I'd rather not be interviewed."

"Come on, can't you tell me something? Why do you do it?"

She sighed and took a breath. "I'm doing it because I love the sport. I played in school. I think it's especially great for kids because everyone plays. No one person can make the team. They have to learn to work together. It's valuable for them to learn."

"So you're doing all this for a neighbor? That's a generous thing to do."

"As I said, I enjoy it. If you'll excuse me, we're going to start."

"Can I talk to you more after the game?" Clark pressed as she turned away.

She glanced at Mark Richards again, but he said nothing. "Actually, I'd rather not, but there's quite a few of the volunteers with really interesting stories. Take our ref, Mr. Green. I played soccer with his youngest daughter. His kids are grown and moved out of state. He has grandkids but can't travel to ref or watch their games. So he gives his time to local children. He's great with the kids. Now, if you'll excuse me, I need to focus on the game."

CR80

Mark found himself watching Jillian almost as much as

he watched the game. She was fascinating. There was no doubt she was giving the boys one hundred percent, no faking her excitement or her approval. There was also no doubt the boys knew it and they gave her their all back. Then again what boy, what child, wouldn't want to do their best when they got the praise and encouragement she was giving? He wasn't surprised when they won, but he knew, even if they didn't, Jillian would still let them know she was proud of them.

The first thing she did at the end of the game was to get the boys around her to give the other team a cheer and shake hands. She then gathered them back together and told each one something good she saw him do.

"See you at practice on Wednesday," she reminded them before they headed to their parents.

"Dad, did you see me score?" Jordan ran toward him.

"Sure did. That was great."

"Yeah, we practiced that move over and over again. And we got it right. And I did my shot just like Jillian told us, for the far pole. It gave me the better angle just like Jillian said it would. Wasn't it wicked?"

"I guess it was." Mark smiled at his son's pleasure. "I'd definitely say you earned going out. What do you want, pizza or burgers?"

"Can I invite one of the guys?"

"I don't see why not, if it's okay with his parents."

"Great. Sam, do you want to go get pizza or burgers with us?"

Mark saw the boy get excited, and then he looked to Jillian. "Can I go? I'm sure Mom would say it was okay, and I'll be done before we have to go get Abby."

The hesitation was obvious, as was wanting to let her charge go with his friend.

"Why don't you join us?" Mark stepped forward.

She looked at him surprised.

"Please." When he smiled, she smiled back, though a

bit timid.

She nodded.

"Good." Inside it felt much more than good. Suddenly, his lunch out with his son, which was always one of his favorite things, just got better.

"I need to get my gear."

"No problem." He folded up his lawn chair and went to stand by her. When she put her clipboard in her bag and zipped it, he reached down and picked it up. "Which way?"

"I can carry it."

"I know you can, but you wouldn't want these boys to miss an example of what a gentleman should do for a lady."

Her lips twitched. "Nicely done, Chief."

"Day off. Mark."

Her lips parted into a smile. "Mark."

Her eyes met his, and he felt the spark of awareness flame to life. There was no stopping his gaze as it drifted over her or the reaction that it brought. It felt good be alive in a male sort of way. Not that he hadn't admired women in the last few years and dated, but this was different. He found himself anxious to find out what the difference was. And he would find out, even if she was involved in a case. Mark knew he couldn't ignore what Jillian Taylor stirred in him. She was too intriguing, and he loved a good intrigue.

The adults followed the boys to where her car was parked, about a dozen spaces from his. "What's it going to be boys?" he asked.

"Pizza." the boys said in unison, the choice already discussed.

"Okay." He turned to Jillian. "There's a pizza place we like not far from where you live, unless you have a place in mind."

"Gio's?"

"You know it."

"I like the stuffed crust BBQ chicken."

"A woman after my own heart, but I'm afraid we'll

have to get a pepperoni for the boys. Listen, how about we drop your car off at your condo, and drive together?"

She shifted. "I have to get Abby after."

"No problem. I know where the clinic is, and it would probably be easier to put her in my SUV."

He could tell the last was a deciding factor. "Are you sure you wouldn't mind her in your car?"

"It's fine."

"Thank you. Sam volunteered to sit with her to keep her down while I drive, but I'd rather sit with her."

"We're set then."

It took only a couple minutes to drive to Jillian's condo. Jordan climbed in the back seat with Sam leaving Jillian to slide into the front seat. The boys immediately started talking excitedly about the game.

As the adults were left out of the conversation, Mark started. "So you played soccer in school?"

"Yes. I started with the youth programs, played on the high school team then my first two years of college."

"Really, why'd you stop?"

"I messed up my knee in the second game of the third year."

Mark pulled up at a stoplight and glanced at her legs. He could barely make out the two tiny white scars on her left knee now that he was so close. It was hard not to look at the total long, beautiful length of them. "How did it happen?" After the question was asked, he cringed realizing that might be something she felt uncomfortable talking about.

"Slide tackle, got me instead of the ball. She caught me from behind. I didn't see it coming, couldn't avoid it. Put me out for the rest of the season."

"And then some." He made the guess.

"Yeah, I was on crutches the whole semester."

"You didn't go out the next year."

"No, I had a large load, trying to get the credits I

needed to graduate, and I was doing an internship that took a lot of time."

"It's too bad you had to give it up."

"Yeah, I miss it. I do love soccer. This has been fun working with the boys. I don't let them slide tackle on my team. Too much chance of them getting hurt or them hurting the other person, and it's not because of what happened to me. I've never liked or used them."

"But you enjoy coaching?"

"Yes, more than I thought I would. I'm glad Sam asked me. I had been helping him practice so he knew all about my playing."

"Well, the boys did great today."

"Yes, they did. I'm very proud of the way they acted. I think they're going to do well together."

Mentally, Mark agreed, but his thoughts shifted to her. "I hope you don't mind if I get nosey, but yesterday when you told me you weren't meeting a date, I got the impression there wasn't anyone special in your life. Is that right?"

She was quiet a second then turned to look at him. There was a challenging look in her eye. "Before I answer, can I ask if this is Mark asking, or the Chief?"

"Mark," he said firmly. "Would it make a difference?"

"No, the answer would be the same, but it will make a difference in what I say next." She brushed back a lock of hair that had slipped from her ponytail.

"Fair enough."

"I'm not dating anyone right now. I've spent a lot of time the last two years getting my business going. I'm not into the bar scene or the casual date thing." She paused again, but this time she seemed to be gathering her courage, which surprised him until her next words came out.

"What about you? Jordan mentioned his parents were divorced, and I understand his mother isn't around."

"We've been split up over six years. And no, I'm not

dating anyone right now. Well, I occasionally go out, but no one regular." He pulled into a parking lot, turning his attention to her.

Her lips were quirked up at the corner.

"What?"

She shook her head. "I don't know. I'm just trying to get the image of you right in my mind. There seem to be a lot of twists, and I can't figure out which is right."

"I'll tell you what. Let's go in and order, send the boys to the arcade next door for twenty minutes, and you can tell me what you've come up with, and I'll tell you how you did."

Five minutes later they settled in a booth by themselves, the boys only too happy to leave them.

"Okay, so you've had a minute to think. Tell me what you've come up with," Mark challenged.

"You love your son."

"Very much, but that's too easy."

"No, I mean, you really love your son. He means the world to you. You'd do anything to protect him. That's why you have him and his mother doesn't."

"Yes, but she wasn't really into motherhood."

Jillian nodded. "So between work, which is also very important to you and Jordan, you don't have a lot of time for yourself. You like it that way. Occasionally, you date a woman, but mainly when it's called for."

She was getting into it now. "Or when a friend sets up a date you can't get out of. Then, if you like the woman, you might go out again until you decide whether she'd fit into your life. It doesn't take you long, only a couple dates to decide, and you end the relationship before you lead her on. You are alone because you've yet to meet the one that's right."

He tilted his head in concurrence. "Very good." He was impressed. "You're not interested in being a detective by chance?"

She laughed. "No thank you. In my business, you have two kinds of decorators. Some go in, do what they want, make these nice little show cases. The others listen to what the client wants and pull it together in a pleasing manner. I try to be the second. I try to listen to and read people."

"You're very good. I have police officers who have known me for years but couldn't come up with what you just did."

"It's because you're a touch of an enigma. There are just some things that don't quite fit."

"Like what?"

"Jordan's mother. You're the faithful sort. You work out problems. The 'marry for true love'."

Mark shifted again surprised at what she saw in a short time. He picked up a straw from the table and rolled it in his fingers.

"I'm sorry," Jillian reacted unconsciously reaching out to put her hand over his.

"No, it's okay." He turned his hand over to catch hers, so they were linked palm to palm. "I admit marrying Jordan's mother was not one of the smartest things I did. It was the timing."

He paused to put the straw in his drink and took a swallow. "I had just come off working narcotics. It was a hard set. You see some of the ugliest parts of police work. It's all there; murder, abuse, just filth. I can't say I was cut out for it. It was a learning experience. One I needed, but not fun. I was new in the detective division, still feeling my way through. Proving I was my own man, not there because daddy pulled strings."

"Your father is a police officer?"

"No, my father was a senator."

"Senator Richards was your father?" she interrupted.

"Yes."

"Oh, my. Your parents were killed in a car accident."

"Yes, five years ago."

"I'm sorry."

"Thank you. Anyway to get on with it, I met Jordan's mother at a fundraiser with my parents. As I said, I'd just come off a bad stint. She was beautiful, elegant, a million miles from what I'd been seeing, and she turned it all on me. After all the ugliness I'd been through, I ate it up. Fell hard for it. We were married within two months. That was when I started to find out what she planned. She thought I'd give up being a cop and go into politics. She thought I was just having my youthful experience and was using it as a stepping stone before I made a bid for mayor, then of course, on to governor or maybe senator, following my father.

"She couldn't believe I could be happy in law enforcement and want to stay in it, and that I didn't mind my 'little' apartment. By three months, I knew it was not good, but then we found out she was expecting. My parents were spending most of their time in Washington, and when not there, they'd go to the cabin so they suggested that we move into their house. That made Felicity happy for a while, though she didn't like that I made her live on a cop's salary. The money was my parents'. It helped that we didn't have to pay rent.

"Anyway, Jordan was born. The house and name kept her in the social class she wanted, so she was happy. She went to all the events, joined the popular charities. Life went on. We were pretty much just existing together, and then she met someone who was what she wanted in the political scene and who had money. She told me she wanted a divorce. When I pressed for shared custody, she gave me full if I helped push the divorce through faster. I did. She remarried a month later and moved to California and is quite happy. She visits Jordan about once a year and sends gifts when she remembers."

"Oh my, how could she not want to see him? He's such a great boy."

"Thank you for that. But it's just not her. What she regretted most was that was when my parents died, I inherited everything, and she couldn't get any of it."

"She actually tried?"

"A brief attempt, but the marriage had been over for almost two years. She had signed full custody to me. I never asked for any child support or anything else. Her suit was rejected pretty quickly."

"She actually thought you'd just pay her so it wouldn't go to court," Jillian speculated.

Again Mark was surprised at her perception. "That's right."

"I'm glad you didn't hand it over."

"So, you don't think I'm a cold, vindictive man?"

She looked deep into his eyes. "No, I don't think she deserves you or Jordan."

"You're only hearing my side of the story."

"Yes, but I think I'll trust your side, Chief Richards."

"Thank you, but now that I've killed the lively mood with that thrilling story, why don't I get the boys? The pizza should be here in a minute." Mark stood before she could answer. Walking away, he couldn't believe he'd told her the whole story. What a date killer. Not that it had been a date, but so much for the likelihood of getting one. He probably sounded like a bitter fool.

CB80

Jillian watched him walk away, fascinated with the man. There was so much to Mark Richards, so much underneath that he hadn't said. He was one of those people who had strong goals and wasn't afraid to do the dirty work to get to them.

He went into law enforcement because it fit his sense of honor. He moved up to police chief because it fit his drive. Not because it was politically expedient, but because that was where he could make a bigger difference. But before getting there, he'd made sure he knew what the departments were all about.

She looked up to see him walking back toward her. Her heart lurched. Dressed in jeans and T-shirt, he looked younger and – wow. His lips rose up at the corner as if he knew her thoughts.

"They'll be here as soon as they defeat the demon horde."

‍‍‍

∞

The pizza was great. The company was better. Mark sighed in contentment. This was the best date he'd been on in years, not that it was a date. Well, actually, it was. He had asked, she had accepted. It was a date, even if it was a spur of the moment thing with two boys.

He also learned one very important thing. Jillian Taylor had no problem being around his son. She didn't act fake with him, didn't try to play up to Jordan to get his interest. She was herself and accepted Jordan just as he was, a ten-year-old boy, who had a burping contest with his new friend at the end of the meal. Mark wanted to hang his head in embarrassment.

Jillian laughed and proceeded to tell the boys about one of her friends on her soccer team who could out-burp any guy, and that on an away trip, their coach threatened to tie her to the goal and let the team take shots at her if she didn't stop. They were all laughing with her when she finished.

When the waitress came over to see if they needed anything else, Mark got the hint that it was time to go. "Shall we?" He held his hand out for her.

"I guess so." She then looked at her watch. "Oh my, I didn't realize. I have to pick up Abby by two."

"We'll make it. Come on boys."

∞

It took twenty minutes to reach the vet's office. They made it with five minutes to spare.

"Sorry I'm late," Jillian said as she rushed in the door.

"No problem," Eliza Jones greeted them. She was a petite woman with a mass of curly brown hair and a lot of energy. "I knew you'd make it, and Abby has just been sleeping. Looks like you brought a crew. Chief Richards," the woman said to Mark on seeing him.

"Dr. Jones," he acknowledged.

"How much do I owe you?" Jillian pulled her wallet out of her purse.

"Oh, it's all been taken care of." The doctor looked at the police chief.

Jillian caught the motion and turned to him. "You paid for her?"

"Let's just say it was taken care of by someone who wanted to remain anonymous."

She eyed him a moment, wondering if he'd covered the bill personally, but his expression gave nothing away.

"You ready to take her home?" the vet asked.

"Oh, yes." Jillian was more than ready. She couldn't believe how much she missed her and it was worse knowing she was hurt. She followed Eliza into the back room where the kennels were.

"She's such a sweetie, very well behaved."

"She is. Oh, there's my baby." Jillian knelt down in front of the kennel. Abby started to whine and wiggle her whole body. "Sit girl." Jillian tried to calm her, but the minute the door was open, Abby burst through into her lap. "That's my girl." Jillian ran her fingers over Abby, careful of the patches that had stitches.

"Hey, Abby." Sam came over to pet her and received a greeting lick.

"You want to come meet her, Jordan? She's friendly." Jillian invited.

"Sure." He dropped down by her and immediately received the same treatment as Sam.

"Abby," Jillian corrected the dog. "She's not supposed to lick people's faces." Jillian caught the dog's head between her hands and lowered her forehead to the top of Abby's. "Ready to go home?" She dodged the tongue, laughed, and pulled the leash from her purse.

With the boys on either side of Abby, they all said good-bye.

Mark opened the tailgate then carefully lifted the dog inside while Jillian got into the back seat.

"If you put the little center piece down, you can reach her easier."

Gratefully, Jillian followed the suggestion. Before the others had even gotten in the car, Abby had her muzzle resting on the arm rest between Jillian and Sam. At her condo, Mark again came around to lift her out so she didn't pull her stitches.

"Thank you for everything." Jillian caught the leash.

"We'll walk you up."

Jillian started to object but thought better of it as Mark raised his eyebrow. "This way."

"Jillian, can Jordan and I stop to see if Mom's home yet?"

She looked to Mark.

"It's fine with me," he said.

"All right, if she's not, come straight back."

They followed the sidewalk around the corner of the clubhouse which sat in front of her building. Jillian's condo was on the end. A small, enclosed patio to the side of the walk was given privacy by a tree and a couple of bushes.

"She seems to be walking fine." Mark looked down at the dog as they approached her condo.

Jillian followed his gaze. "Yes, Dr. Jones said she was fortunate. Though she had lots of stitches, the cuts were fairly shallow. It's a good thing Abby has a nice thick coat. There wasn't too much muscle damage. Eliza said she'll heal fast, probably be back to normal in a couple of weeks. The only thing is, she'll likely have a lighter streak of fur where the cuts were. I can handle that, considering I feel lucky to still have her." She leaned over slightly to run her hand over the dog's head.

The man popped up from behind the bushes by her patio.

Surprised, Jillian shrieked. Abby crouched and growled, and Mark stepped in front of them as a shield – all at the same time.

The figure cried out and fell back over a flower pot. Mark sprang forward, grabbed the man by his shirt front, and pulled him up. A second later, Mark had one arm pinned behind the struggling man's back.

It happened so fast, it took Jillian's brain a second to catch up and recognize the man. "Mark, let him go." She dropped the leash and rushed up, catching Mark's arm. "Let him go." She eased his hand away. "It's all right. Toby, are you all right?" She helped the man straighten.

The man-boy looked past her. "Who is he?" Toby glared at Mark.

"He's a friend."

"Why did he jump on me?"

"You startled me. When I yelled, Mark went to protect me. I'm sorry." She tried to explain.

"I would never hurt you, Jillian."

"I know. I'm sorry." She patted his hand. "Are you okay?"

He nodded and sent another glare at Mark.

"What are you doing here Toby?"

"I brought Abby a bone. The butcher said I could have it. I asked."

"That was very nice of you."

"Did Abby get hurt?" He knelt down by the dog, obviously nervous to touch her because of the bandages.

"Yes. I'm just bringing her home from the vet. It's okay to pet her, just be careful."

"Did he hurt her?" There was no mistaking the hostility as Toby glared at Mark.

"No, he's a friend," Jillian said soothingly. "He was helping me bring her home. His name is Mark. Mark, this is Toby."

"Hello, Toby. I'm sorry I handled you so roughly. I thought you were going to hurt Jillian."

"I would never hurt her."

"I can see that now. I was just trying to protect her."

"I can protect Jillian. She doesn't need you to protect her."

"That's nice of you, but it's what I do. I protect people. I'm a police officer."

The look in Toby's eyes changed to one of excitement. "A real policeman? Do you carry a gun?"

"Yes, but it's in its lockbox right now. I'm off duty. I was at a soccer game with my son."

The look that came over Toby was one of relief. "Is he on Jillian's soccer team?"

"Yes."

"I'm going to be Jillian's special helper sometimes. If I listen to what Jillian says," the man announced importantly.

"That's good of you."

The boys came running up. "Mom's home," Sam announced. "She said we could play a video game if it was okay with his Dad."

"Is it okay Dad? Just for a minute."

Mark looked to Jillian. "Do you mind the company? All in the name of the boys' new friendship," he added for extra pull.

"The boys' friendship?" Her lips twitched. She eyed him speculatively.

"Well, maybe for ours, too." The glint in his grin was unmistakable.

Jillian felt her heart leap in recognition. "All right."

"Okay." Mark turned his son. "Go play for a while, but not too long. You don't want to overstay your welcome."

The boys raced off again. Jillian realized Toby was

still standing there. He eyed Mark curiously.

"Toby, would you like a drink or something? We could sit out here on the patio."

He shifted back and forth then glanced at his watch. "Oh, no. I have to get back to work." There was hesitation in his movements. "I just wanted to bring Abby the bone." He pointed where a bag lay in front of the sliding glass door. "I better get back. Bye, Jillian." He looked again at Mark, his eyebrows pulling together in a slight frown. "Bye, Officer Mark."

"Bye, Toby."

They stood as the man ran off. As soon as they were inside, Jillian put food and fresh water down for Abby.

"You have an admirer," Mark commented from the doorway to the kitchen.

"Yes, I'm not sure what to do about it. Toby is very sweet, and I don't want to hurt him. I try to just be his friend, but I'm afraid he has a crush."

"Does he live around here?"

"Somewhere a couple streets over, I think. He works at the grocery store across the park."

"Where Sandra Cannon works?"

"Yes, he's a bagger. Would you like some juice? I don't keep pop around."

"Water's fine."

"How about some ice cream?"

"Now, that is something you can tempt me with."

⊙ఠ⊙

Later that night, Mark lay back on his bed and thought of Jillian. She had hardly been out of his mind. He owed his son. The minute of game play had lasted over an hour and a half. And, like his son said, the time had gone fast.

He and Jillian had sat on the couch, eaten ice cream and talked about anything and everything. She had painting the picture on her wall, a hobby she hadn't much time for in the last few years, but she did try to keep up. He wondered what it would take to get her to do him a painting. He knew she didn't think he was serious when he asked.

He sighed, as his mind pulled up the image of her. She really had great legs, oh yeah, and such a nice body, but those eyes, those beautiful telling eyes. Looking into them, he found the real Jillian. Her eyes showed just what she thought or felt. She was all there, totally open if you just looked. He liked that. He liked a lot of what he found out today. He couldn't wait to find out more. He sighed again and closed his eyes, letting the excitement of what was to come roll over him.

There was more to come.

⚬⚬⚬

Jillian came out of the bathroom and smiled at the dog lying on her pillow next to the bed. Abby knew she wasn't allowed on the furniture, but she had kept as close to Jillian as she could all evening, which was just fine with her. She needed the contact.

"Good night, girl." She knelt down to stroke the Lab. "It's so nice to have you home." She wrapped her arms around the dog, burying her face into the soft, sun-colored fur. Happily she felt the soft tongue on her shoulder beside the strap of her thin nightgown. She leaned back looking down at the dog.

"Well, at least I get some kisses tonight. I wonder what it would be like to be kissed good night by Police Chief Richards. He's a seriously good-looking man. Like no man I've ever dated. Yes, I know it wasn't a date. But that is more time than I've spent with a man who wasn't holding a paintbrush, hammer, or other building tool in a long time." She rubbed Abby under her chin.

"I swear, in college, all the boys were after three things: the next party, thrill, or girl. I know Cynical, I know, after a couple bad experiences. A lot of it was my own fault. I was always such a tomboy that the guys I liked thought of me as just one of the guys. Still −" She let it hang. "Good night."

She ruffled Abby's fur around her neck and climbed into bed, trying not to look toward the window. No matter how hard she refused to let the darkness outside her condo get to her, the unease was there in the back of her mind.

Last night's sleep had come after exhaustion had finally claimed her. Tonight, she looked to the window. The curtains were pulled tight over the sliding glass doors, but the darkness still edged around the fan above. With a mental shake, she drew her eyes away. She was safe. There was nothing out there to get her. He couldn't know where she lived.

⋒

He stood behind the bushes at the corner of the clubhouse. The lights that glowed up from the swimming pool didn't draw his attention. It was focused on the light coming from the second floor of the condo on the end. Beauty was there. He'd watched as the lights downstairs had turned off and the ones upstairs came on.

On the roof a patch glowed up like a beacon from the skylight that he guessed was in her bathroom. If he were on her roof, he could look down at her. He could see her. He made up his mind to climb up. He could do it. He could scale any heights for his Beauty. He stepped forward, and the light went out. He pulled back into the shadows.

That was all right. It wasn't time to go to her yet. She needed to learn to love him first so she could see past the beast. So she could set him free from the curse. He'd watch and wait. He could do that. He was good at that. His Beauty would love him.

The lights behind the curtains went out.

"Good night, Beauty."

Chapter Six

"Dad, look, my picture's in the paper!" Jordan exclaimed excitedly, running into the kitchen. "See the pass from Sam and the score." He held the paper out so the four-by-eight picture was up. There, in full color, was a clear picture of the two boys just as Jordan kicked the ball into the goal.

"Hey, all right. We'll have to cut it out for your scrapbook."

"I'll get the scissors."

Mark studied at the picture. It really was a good shot, great clarity. "What?" He cut back the curse, but the word hung like venom as he stared at the picture and the blonde-haired woman shown clearly in the background, clipboard in hand, cheering on her team.

So clear that the predator could recognize her instantly.

Mark read down the article about the players and the need for volunteers. Clark wrote about the old ref, Raymond, who helped out other people's kids because he couldn't go to his own grandchildren's games. He turned a couple pages to continue the story, fighting to keep from swearing.

Anyone can find the time to volunteer, even one of the

area's leading interior designers. A young woman of grace and beauty donned a whistle and picked up a clipboard to coach a neighbor boy's team when they lost their coach, though she has no children of her own. Her team did great, but who wouldn't do their best for a long-legged beauty like that? I'll bet there are a lot of men out there that would love to be her assistant, and the organization can use all the volunteers they can get.

He was going to ring a reporter's neck. But first he'd have to pay a visit to Jillian Taylor and not the casual, fun meeting he'd been planning on.

Jordan came back with the scissors, and Mark forced down his frustration while they read, then cut out the article together. Jordan jabbered on excitedly.

"What do you think about going over and showing Jillian and Sam, just in case they didn't see it yet?" Mark suggested, keeping the smile on his face.

"You mean it?"

"Sure. In fact, why don't you grab your swimsuit, and maybe we can talk Jillian into letting you swim while I talk with her."

"All right. Maybe Sam can swim, too."

"You can see."

Jordan ran off. Mark paced the room then picked up the phone. Pulling a card from his wallet, he punched in the number. "Nigel Clark, please," he said when a woman answered.

"I'm sorry, he isn't in today."

"Will you give me his number, please?"

"I'm sorry. I can't give out that information."

"This is Police Chief Mark Richards." He paused for emphasis. "Give me that number."

"I ... I'm sorry sir. I can't. Its policy, but he should be at his desk at nine o'clock in the morning."

He debated pressing it but heard the sound of footsteps on the stairs. "Thank you." He put the phone down, vowing that he would be seeing a certain reporter at nine o'clock sharp.

They made one short stop on the way to Jillian's to buy another newspaper. Getting through the security gate wasn't any trouble. They just followed the car in front of them through before the gate closed.

Jillian's doorbell was answered first with one bark from Abby and about five seconds later by Jillian. Her hair was pulled back in a ponytail again, but today, her face was totally free of makeup. The bruise on her chin was clearly visible, though it had faded to a yellowish green.

"Mark, Jordan." her surprise was obvious.

Abby, recognizing them, settled down on the floor by the unlit fireplace.

"Did you see it?" Jordan burst out excited.

"See what?" She looked from him to Mark.

"We made the paper."

"What?"

"See, Sam and I are in the paper." He held it up for her to see.

"Oh, wow. Look at that. What a shot and I'm talking about your kick, not the picture. That's so cool. I haven't even looked at the paper yet. I think I may have to frame it."

"Do you think Sam has seen it?"

"I don't know, but I doubt it because he hasn't been over here, yet."

"Do you have a paper?" Mark entered the conversation finally.

Jillian looked to him, her brow wrinkling. She nodded and glanced to the table where the paper sat waiting for her to take time to look at it.

Mark dropped his hand on Jordan's shoulder. "Why don't you go see Sam? You can also see if it's okay for you guys to go for a swim, if that's okay with Jillian?" His eyes never left her.

She shifted under his gaze. "Sure, we'll just have to go sit poolside and watch them."

"I brought dad's suit so we can all swim."

That brought Mark's attention from her to his son, but Jillian's next words took it right back. "That sounds like fun. Why don't you go see if Sam can join us?"

Jordan dropped the backpack he'd been carrying with the swimsuits and ran out.

"You didn't know he brought your swimsuit?"

"No."

"You wanted to talk to me?" There was hesitancy in Jillian's voice that hadn't been there when he left the evening before, as if she sensed the impending doom.

"Yeah." He walked to the table, picked up the paper, pulling the rubber band from it. He drew out the section with the picture and turned it to her. "Take a closer look."

She stepped next to him.

"Look past the boys." When he heard her intake of breath, he knew she was seeing herself there for the first time.

Fear was clear in her features when she looked to him. "You don't think there's anything to worry about?"

He knew she was looking for assurance. He wished he could give it, but he just felt too uneasy himself. "Probably not, but you'd better read the article."

Her hand settled on the paper next to his. His pulse jumped when she brushed against him as she moved to read. He tried to tell himself that it was the desire to protect her but he knew different. It was just plain desire that ached through him. He tightened the reins on his control until she turned to him. Her face drained of color.

"He all but said my name." The shaky words destroyed his resolve. He dropped the paper and had her in his arms before it landed on the table. Jillian clung to him, burying her head in his chest. Her trembling was painful to feel. He wanted to make it go away. He wished he had never shown her the paper, though he knew she needed to be made aware.

"I'm not going to let anything happen to you." The vow came out loud, but it was made to himself. He ran his hand up and down her back in an effort to soothe her. Jillian was his responsibility now, his to watch over.

Mark shifted back, raising his hand to her cheek to tilt her head up to him. "I'm sorry. But I wanted you to know. So we can take precautions. Just to be on the safe side. Chances are the perpetrator will never see the newspaper or put it together. But we have to be prepared just in case."

Her eyes searched his face, obviously finding reassurance there because she relaxed and nodded. She didn't move from his arms and he couldn't release her, unable to get away from those clear, lake-blue eyes. The feel of her became imprinted along the length of him. His heart raced and he could feel hers match beats. Her head tilted to him as he lowered his.

"Jillian," her name slipped out in a whisper, just an inch from her lips. He closed the space.

"Sam can go." Jordan burst through the door. Mark jerked back just as Jillian did. Five feet separated them before Jordan turned to see them in the kitchen.

"Great, there's a bathroom right there." She pointed to the other side of the dining nook. "You can change there, and I'll get my suit on." Her hands interlocked together then twisted in a nervous fashion. "I'll be right back." She ran up the stairs.

⚜

Jillian stopped just inside her bedroom door and collapsed back against the wall. She couldn't believe what just about happened. She'd almost kissed Mark Richards. Her heart thundered in her chest. She could still feel his arms around her. She tried to tell herself that he had done it only to comfort her, but even she couldn't mistake the look on his face. It was hot, full of desire.

If Jordan had come in one second later, he would have seen his coach kissing his father. And she wanted to kiss him, more than she'd ever wanted anything. She felt flushed. She had almost convinced herself what she had been feeling for him was gratitude, security, frustration. Well, all those things were there, but there was something deeper, something more. Something she'd never experienced before.

She was drawn to Mark Richards. Not just looks and lusting after a good-looking man. This wasn't the same. Not that Mark wasn't good looking − he was, and extremely appealing to her, but her feelings for him were from deep in her heart. It was a shake the world feeling that frightened and excited her.

The question was − what to do about it?

She dropped her head to her hands and drew in a deep breath. Right now, she'd put on her swimming suit and join him and his son at the pool like nothing had happened to tilt her world. Oh, heavens, she'd have to go before him in a swimsuit. It was okay. She could do it. She had a good body.

Jillian pushed away from the wall, going to pick out a suit. She stared down helpless, what she didn't own was one of those suits meant to catch a man's eye. Hers were more the utilitarian type, plain one piece meant for swimming laps. Well, she wasn't trying to catch Mark's eye. She was swimming with his son. She picked out her newest suit, a light teal, and went to change.

A second later, she stood in front of the mirror and tried again to catch her breath. Okay, she looked good, she conceded. She was making too much out of this. So what if he almost kissed her? She'd been kissed before, just maybe not as often as most women her age. But, she'd been a late bloomer, a tomboy and just too busy. She was an adult now, a successful business woman. She could handle a man desiring her.

What if he didn't? What if it was all her? What if she'd read the situation wrong? With a groan, she turned to get some beach towels. She was going insane.

Father and son were waiting for her as she came down the stairs. Jordan sat on the floor by Abby. Abby's chin rested on his thigh.

She smiled at the boy. "She's not very active, yet." The sight of the dog brought reality back. "She's still sore, and the medication Dr. Jones gave her makes her sleepy." Jillian went over to the dog and bent down to stroke Abby's head. "You be a good girl, and we'll be back soon."

Jillian stood, looking back to Mark, letting herself get her first good look at him. She totally forgot the newspaper article as her heart lurched once more. He was a handsome man. His sandy-brown hair was brushed back carelessly. His shoulders were broad. The muscles of his chest and abdomen were well-defined. His skin was tanned with a sprinkling of darker hair. His suit came almost to his knees, but still showed a pair of nice, masculine legs.

The knock on the door pulled her attention from the man before she could do something foolish like an old-fashion swoon.

"That'll be Sam. Let's go." She drew in a deep breath as she opened the door.

CRBO

Mark was having a hard time keeping from staring at Jillian. She was beautiful. All long lines and tantalizing curves. Her one piece suit might be considered modest, but oh, did it hug her contour nicely. The color set off the golden tan of her skin, and made her eyes pick up an almost green tint in the blue. She moved with an athletic grace that was … oh, wow. He wanted so much to span her narrow waist with his hands. Lift her up over his head and let her slide down in his arms. She wasn't delicate. She was lithe, strong and perfect.

He tried to force his thoughts back to a safer level.

What was he thinking? He couldn't get involved with her. He was the police chief and she was his witness. They'd met in the line of work. True, he'd have met her anyway as Jordan's coach, which probably wasn't much better.

He should back off. Then he thought about almost kissing her. He'd been going to. There was no denying it. And, there was no denying she was going to let him kiss her. He'd seen the desire in her eyes. He felt another rush of excitement, which escalated when he let his eyes linger over her again.

He jerked himself back. She was not only involved in a case, but he was almost ten years older than her, way too old for her. He wasn't the cradle-robber type. Okay, so it wouldn't be cradle-robbing, but ten years. That was too much. Five, six, maybe even seven, but ten? Well, not quite ten. He watched as Jillian turned to catch the ball Jordan threw to her in a game of keep away. Her body came up out of the water as she leapt to make the catch.

Okay, so what were a few more years? Mark forgot all about their ages and took off after her with powerful strokes. His arm snaked around her waist, and exhilaration coursed through him even though she got the ball off before he had time to grab it from her. He felt he won the greater prize. She was laughing when she turned in his arms then they both went down under the water and came up gasping. She broke free.

Water spiked her eyelashes, framing the playful glint in her eyes. She laughed, swimming away to be in position to receive the throw from whomever he tried to get the ball from.

After a half hour play, the adults conceded the game and moved to the loungers to sit.

"That was fun." Jillian sighed.

"They wore you out."

She shook her head. "You should see soccer practice. There, they wear me out."

"This probably wasn't how you planned to spend your day."

"Actually, I really didn't have much planned, just time with Abby. I'm going to keep her close for a few days. I'll take her to work with me tomorrow. She stays in the back room or in a kennel out back. Nan spoils her when I'm not around. Sneaks her treats like I don't know what's happening."

When a shadow of unease crossed Jillian's face, Mark guessed where her thoughts had turned.

"I don't want you going anywhere alone. I don't want you in the shop alone."

"Do you really think he might come after me?" She frowned and he had to resist the urge to reach for her.

"I don't know. I plan to talk with the psychologist who's been working on the profile for us tomorrow, and see what he says. I just wish that picture hadn't ended up in the paper." He knew his frustration came through his voice.

"I'll be careful," she promised.

"I want you to be more than that. I want you to be extra observant. I'm not trying to make you paranoid, but you watch everyone around you. And, put my number on speed dial − first one that comes up. If anything happens, I want you to call me. If you even so much as feel you're being followed, call nine-one-one."

He could see what he said disturbed her, but she nodded.

"Man, I'm sure not making points toward getting to take you out, am I?" he grumbled derisively.

"You want to take me out?" This time it wasn't fear that widened her eyes.

He let a touch of wickedness play across his face. "Yeah, I thought about it. I have to ask you something first."

"What's that?"

"Do you think I'm too old for you?"

"Too old?" Her stunned expression was a stroke to his ego, as were her next words. "You're not old at all."

"Jordan was already born when I was your age." He felt it his duty to point out.

"You're not old." She glanced away. A blush lit her cheeks. "I'd like to go out with you."

"Good, now the problem is when. As you pointed out yesterday, between work and Jordan, I don't have a lot of free time. And, as much as I love my son, I want a date with just the two of us."

Her blush deepened. "I have soccer practice on Wednesday and Friday this week. Next week it will go down to only Wednesday."

"How about Tuesday night? Can we try for that? I'll have to phrase it that way because I never know what will come up."

"Okay."

"Oh, wait a minute I can't do it Tuesday. I have a council meeting. How about Thursday?"

"Thursday's fine."

"Good." He lounged back. He had a date with Jillian. He felt like a teenage boy who'd just scored a date with the prom queen.

"Sam!" Sam's mom called from outside the fence. "Time to get ready to go."

Jillian glanced at the clock on the back wall of the clubhouse. "Oh, my, I didn't realize how much time had passed. Mrs. Morris will have your dinner waiting for you."

"Actually, Mrs. Morris has the weekends off, so we fend for ourselves. We either have leftovers, eat out, or we grill. I can handle grilling. You wouldn't like to join us by chance? We can stop and get some steaks at the store. Maybe pick up a movie."

There was a look of yearning on her face, but she shook her head. "I think I'd better stay with Abby."

"Bring her," he suggested.

"Not yet. She's still not up to being shifted around much."

After a slight hesitation, she spoke again. "How about we put a couple baking potatoes in the oven then go over to the store, get the steaks, bring them back here and I'll grill them for you. That is, if you don't have to get Jordan home."

"No, we're free and I'd like that." He fought down the pleasure that burst within him, afraid he'd scare her. It was a simple dinner with his son around, but it felt like more. "If it won't be an imposition."

"Not at all. I'd like the company. We might even find some corn on the cob for dinner."

"That sounds great. Jordan, what do you think of letting Jillian fix us dinner?"

"Cool."

Twenty five minutes later, after showering, changing, then leaving Jordan behind with Abby, Jillian watched Mark pick out a couple steaks. "You know, I'm never going to be able to eat a steak that large."

"This one is for Abby, but if you're nice, she might let you share."

"Oh." Her lips twitched into a smile.

"You don't mind her getting some scraps do you? This is kind of a special treat. I promised her a steak for being such a good dog."

"I don't give her much people food, but this I'll allow. You're right. She definitely earned it."

"Agreed," Mark said then his gaze shifted beyond her and his face hardened.

"Mark, is something wrong?" She looked around but didn't see anything.

"What, oh, no. I just saw someone I need to speak to. If you'll excuse me a moment?" His attention had already shifted again. Waves of tension seeped off him.

"Sure. No problem. I'll just go see about the corn."

"I'll meet you there." He was already striding away before he finished the sentence.

Chapter Seven

"What are you doing here?" Mark snapped.

"What? Oh, Richards." Nigel Clark turned his attention from the package of noodles he was holding.

"I asked what you're doing here," Mark demanded.

"It's a grocery store. I would say that's obvious. Got to admit, though, I'm surprised to see you at the store."

"I didn't know you lived close to here."

"Not too far away, and I was on my way home from visiting a friend."

"What friend?"

"A lady friend. What's this, an interrogation?"

"I wanted to talk to you. I told you no picture of Jillian in the paper."

"Jillian? Oh yeah, the long-legged beauty. I didn't."

Mark got the feeling the denial was too casual to be true. He studied the man a minute. "Come with me." He led Clark to the front of the store where there was a stack of newspapers. Mark picked up one, opening it. "Now, you want to tell me you don't know anything about this?" He shoved the article toward the reporter. "You disclosed everything there but her name."

Clark made a show of looking down. "Hey, they must

have changed the picture. It's not the one I had tagged for the article, but this is a much better shot."

The man was a good liar, but Mark had no doubt he was lying. "What are you playing at here, Clark?"

"I don't know what you're talking about."

"Then, I'll spell it out for you. If I find out that you're following Jillian Taylor around and that you are setting her up to try to draw in the killer just so you can get a story or try to catch this guy on your own, you'll find your butt in jail. And, your freedom of speech will not protect you from obstruction of justice and reckless endangerment, or whatever I can find to add on it."

"And you're not sticking close to Miss Taylor hoping she might lead you to the killer?" The reporter probed back, as much as admitting he'd been observing Jillian.

"My reasons are my own. Now, back off." He scowled at the man, wishing he could throw him into a cell right then. He didn't like Clark, nor did he trust him.

"Hey, you can't tell me where to go. This is a free country."

"Yeah, but if you keep following Miss Taylor, she can press a stalking charge and I'll see it enforced. In fact, I'll even help her fill out the paperwork. Now, get your groceries and get out, and I better not see you following her again." Mark turned, leaving the threat hanging and strode off to find Jillian.

☙❧

Jillian had three ears of bi-colored corn that promised to be sweet and a container of large, ripe strawberries that caught her eye. She wondered if Mark and Jordan would like a chocolate dipped strawberry, or was that just a girl thing? Her brothers liked them, but they'd eat anything. She saw peaches and paused. Would guys prefer peaches? She put the basket down to look at them. They were as hard as rocks so that ended the debate.

She reached down for the basket, taking the handle just

as a hand locked on her arm. Startled, Jillian let out a small shriek, stumbling back into the peach bin. She spun to grab the fruit she knocked loose from the stack. Toby pressed next to her, helping hold back the fruit with his large hands. Miraculously, only one peach slipped free and fell to the floor.

"I'm sorry, Jillian." Toby mumbled as she fixed the stack.

"It's okay, Toby. I didn't see you. You just need to let me know you're around before you do something like that." She noticed her hand still trembled slightly but she managed to force a smile to her face.

"I'm sorry. I don't mean to scare you." His voice dropped like a chastened child.

"I know. I've just been a little jumpy lately, and you walk very quietly."

"My mom told me not to clomp everywhere. I practiced so I wouldn't."

"You walk very well."

"She said, just because I was a big man, I didn't need to be like a bull in the china closet." He looked back at the peaches and blushed.

"That wasn't your fault. I knocked them over." She reached out to lay her hand on his arm to reassure him.

"Are you jumpy because of what happened to Sandy?"

"A little."

"I heard you were there that night. That was how Abby got hurt."

"Yes."

"Sandy still hasn't woke up yet. I like her. She always tells me jokes, and she says I'm handsome."

"You are handsome, and I like Sandy too. I called her father this morning. He said she was showing improvement today. They hope she'll wake up soon."

"I hope so. I want her to come back to work."

Jillian smiled. It sounded like she had a rival for

Toby's affections.

"I came to tell you I saw your picture in the paper with your soccer team," he exclaimed shifting side to side. For Jillian, it brought a touch of dread, but Toby didn't notice. He continued talking. "I cut it out and put it on my wall next to the picture of Sandy. She was in the paper last month."

"I remember."

"She saved the little girl. That was scary. I thought the girl was going to die, but Sandy saved her. It was cool. And you saved Sandy, that's cool too."

"It was Abby who saved her and me."

"Are you going to give Abby a steak?" He pointed to the basket.

"Maybe a little."

"That's a lot of steak."

"I'm having company for dinner."

A scowl creased Toby's brow, then deepened as he looked past her. Jillian turned to see Mark coming toward her.

"I got to get back to work," Toby mumbled and grabbed up the peach that had landed on the floor and fled.

"Bye, Toby," Jillian barely got the words out before he disappeared through the swinging door to the stock room.

"I take it I have a way with people today," Mark said as he stopped beside her.

"Pardon?" She looked him over. He seemed a little tense as he stared toward where Toby disappeared.

"Nothing. You seem to get a lot of people popping up in your life."

"You mean like you?" She smiled, thinking she liked that he kept showing up.

A smile came to his lips as if maybe he liked that thought, too. "Actually, I was thinking about Toby."

"But, he's been around awhile. He wanted to let me know he saw the picture in the paper." Jillian didn't realize how in tune with Mark she was until she sensed the slight change in him. She knew he was concerned for her. It made her feel like he truly cared. Not just because his job was to serve and protect. "You're the only man I know who has been reappearing in my life recently."

A twinkle sparked in his eyes. "And is that a good thing?" He moved closer.

Jillian's pulse jumped with awareness. "I'm beginning to think that it might be."

"Let me know when you decide." His head tilted toward her, and she lost all ability to think. Breathless, she parted her lips slightly in anticipation then jumped at a loud crash. She spun around and became aware that not only the women whose carts had run into each other were staring at them, but so was about every other person in the produce department.

"I think we'd better get out of here." Mark grabbed up the basket. "You all done?"

"Yes."

"Good." He caught her hand, leading her to the front.

After paying for the food, he hustled her to the car. Jillian figured he was embarrassed, she knew she was. She was going to kiss him right in the middle of the produce department. She couldn't believe it.

He drove in steely silence and she wondered if he was mad. He turned on to her street just as she couldn't take the tension any longer. "Mark."

He swung the car to the curb and shoved the shift into park. "How can kissing you be so hard? I swear between my son and," he burst out, letting the sentence hang as he reached over the console and pulled her to him.

She pitied anyone who disturbed him right then, Jillian thought an instant before his mouth closed over hers then all she could think of was him. He invaded her senses, seeped into her soul and settled in to stay. She heard him groan and answered with one of her own as pleasure like she'd never experienced rocked her. She didn't know kissing could be like this. But it wasn't just kissing. It was claiming. Certain of only one thing, she knew Mark Richards had just made her his.

His lips left her mouth to caress across her cheek. His hands held her head to angle it for his kiss. "How did that happen?" His voice was heavy in a hoarse growl.

"I don't know," Jillian whispered in awe. "It never happened to me before. I mean." She broke off, suddenly flustered. Not sure what she was going to say.

Luckily, he took over for her, pressing his lips back to hers once more, before settling back into his seat. He gripped the steering wheel so hard his knuckles went white. Tilting his head back, he shut his eyes tight.

She didn't know what to do, what to say. The last time she said his name he kissed her. In all honesty, she wished he would again, but it was certainly the wrong time and place. Still, there was nothing else to say. "Mark?"

He opened his eyes and looked at her, his gaze heated. He kept his hands locked on the wheel. "I'm sorry, Jillian. Please say I didn't scare you."

She shook her head. Scared was the last thing she'd been. "You didn't scare me," she managed to get out breathlessly. "I've just never been kissed like that before."

"That makes two of us." He looked away then back. "I'm trying to tell myself it was the anticipation of wanting it so much. But I don't think that's true." He looked back at her. "I've never felt such a reaction. I don't want you to feel that's a line, because it's not. I don't use them."

"I know," she whispered, reaching to touch his arm.

"Don't." He winced. "Sorry, I'm trying to get myself in control. I'm feeling very primitive here. I'd like to throw you over my shoulder, haul you back to my cave, and claim you as mine."

His choice of the word claim hit her, because it was right out of her thoughts.

He winced, "I didn't mean to shock you. You're safe, I promise. You don't have anything to fear. I'll never hurt you. I'm making this worse. I better shut up now before you start yelling for the police."

She felt a tinge of humor at what he said, and it widened at his obvious discomfort. "I won't have to yell too loud, as you're right here."

He stared at her a moment before he got that she was referring to him, and she wasn't worried. "I just want to say that I felt something when I kissed you."

Jillian decided she didn't want him to get away easy. "Good, because you just rocked my world like no one else has." She left him to think about that. "We better go get those steaks going. Your son and my dog are waiting."

That pulled Mark back to reality for the time being, but he was still thinking of rocking her world later that night as he lay in bed. Her world was definitely not the only one rocked. He could still taste her, ambrosia. He was in so much trouble. He never thought of a woman made just for him, but he knew, if there was one, it was Jillian.

He pictured her in his mind and sighed with pleasure. She smiled at something Jordan said in an easy, relaxed way. The next image was after he brought her up out of the water, locked in his arms, laughter lit her face. The vision changed to right after he'd kissed her, if that could be classified as just a kiss. Her eyes were pools of azure light. Her lips had been full and pink from his attention to them. They were parted as she tried to catch the breath he'd taken.

He experienced a surge of pleasure at being able to put the dazed expression on her face. He knew she'd been caught as unprepared by the response as he had.

The phone ripped him from his reverie, and he sprang to get it. "Richards," he said in the phone.

"Sorry to call you so late," Detective Andrew Hamilton said, giving proof to the wave of unease he sensed the moment the phone rang.

"What's wrong?"

"I thought you'd want to know. It looks like there was a possible attempt on Sandra Cannon tonight."

"What?" He sat up straighter, swinging his legs off the bed.

"I'm at the hospital now. A nurse saw a man, dressed as an orderly, looking like he was trying to sneak into intensive care. She was suspicious because no one should have been coming in then, and he seemed like he was averting his face. And of course, she knew what happened to Sandra. She called out to him and he ran. She alerted security, but they couldn't find him. We've got a man posted at every exit, but I think he's already gone."

"Was the nurse able to give you a description?"

"Just height and build, she didn't get a look at his face."

"What about security cameras?"

"So far no, but I'm still checking," Andrew assured him. "We'll go over them frame by frame. I just wanted to let you know what was happening first."

"I appreciate that. I want an officer stationed right outside Sandra's room."

"I knew you would. Casey's already in place. I'll have a relief assigned before I punch out tonight."

"Sounds like you don't need me," Mark commented drily.

"Not tonight. I just knew you'd have my head if I didn't let you know. Now you do, so you can get some sleep. I'll be here a couple hours and leave a couple extra officers for security to be on the safe side. I doubt he'll be back."

"I agree, still go with the extra security, and I'm going to put a permanent officer on her door. I'll stop by the hospital first thing in the morning. Can you leave your report on my desk? You can have someone drop it off, if needed."

"Will do," the detective answered back.

"Thanks, Andrew."

"Sure thing."

The phone disconnected, and Mark lay back in the bed. This time, his thoughts were on a far less pleasant subject. He didn't like the thought that the killer had gone after Sandra Cannon. The psychologist figured he wouldn't. They were going to have to rethink this, but he didn't like where it was heading. He really didn't like what it hinted for Jillian. She might not have been the killer's intended victim … he started to reach for the phone then stopped.

His wanting to hear her voice was not due to the possible danger. So far, there was no evidence of that, and at the moment, she'd be asleep like he should be. Her doors would be locked, security system set, and the odds were against the killer making another attempt tonight. Odds were also, he didn't even know who Jillian was. Still, Mark decided, he would pay her a visit tomorrow just for his own peace of mind.

CBEO

The man slipped into the darkened house. Rage seeped from his rigid form. Why he had ever gone to the hospital. The woman there was obviously not the one. She was not his Beauty. She would never see past the ugliness to love him. She was not worth his time, and though she didn't deserve to live, he had to forget about her. He needed to concentrate on Beauty. He'd found her now. He was certain of it.

Jillian Taylor was his Beauty. He clenched the metal frame of the camera into his hand. He could bring the image of her up clearly in his mind. He crept through the kitchen and down the hall to the bedroom that would be hers when he brought her there to live with him.

It was the perfect room for his Beauty, from the white wallpaper with tiny red roses, to the wrought iron bed with

91

its filmy draped canopy and white spread with the embroidered roses. It was just like the picture in his book. He could see Jillian here, even without looking at the pictures on the wall surrounding the computer. She would love him and the curse would be over. He would no longer be a beast.

Hideous beast. His mother's words came back to haunt him. Just like your father. No woman would want you. No woman will ever see past the beast. No. No. "No!" He slammed his fist against the wall. Beauty could love him. She could see past the beast he hid. He pulled the wig from his head and touched the rough, scarred patches there. She would love him. She could save him.

He dragged in a breath. First, he had to keep his attention on the task at hand. He removed the memory card from the camera and placed it in the computer. A second later the pictures came up, and with a touch of a button, they began to print, bringing the images to life. She was there in the store, a package of meat in her hand, smiling back over her shoulder at the top cop. Fierce anger sliced through him at the sight of the man.

He would not have time to court his Beauty slowly. He would have to move fast before the cop could move in and steal her away. No, the cop couldn't take his Beauty. Rage flared. The cop could confuse her though, keep her from seeing past the beast.

He picked up the scissors, cutting the police chief away. When he added the pictures to the others of her on the wall, he was the one she was smiling back at.

Chapter Eight

"You have a secret admirer." Nan's voice greeted Jillian as she walked through the door. "Or is he not so mysterious?"

"What?" Jillian looked at her assistant, releasing Abby's leash so the dog could go to the woman, who held out a treat for her.

"How are you girl?" Nan rubbed the dog in greeting. "Look at you all bandaged up, but you look good and you're walking fine. Maybe not as much wiggle in your body."

Jillian smiled as she watched Abby lap up the attention. "She's doing well. Acting more like her normal self, though she does seem to want to stay close."

"Then we'll just keep you close." Nan stroked Abby's head, looking down into her big, brown puppy eyes. "Now, for you." Nan shifted her gaze to Jillian and motioned to the single red rose in a vase on the desk. "It was leaning against the door when I got here. So, are you going to tell me who it is? I can't see one of your soccer boys giving you a rose."

Jillian moved to the flower to take a smell as she thought back over her weekend. Would Mark have left her a flower? She didn't know, but a little rush went through her at the thought. He seemed the more direct type. Not that he wouldn't give flowers, but if he did, he would do it personally. Still, she took another smell of the rose and wondered.

"Okay, I see that smile. You met someone this weekend. When and where did this happen?"

"Well …" Jillian flushed and became tongue tied.

"Come on, Sweet Pea, give! Where did you meet a man? You went to your soccer game. By the way, I saw your picture in the paper. You can tell me about that later. After the game, you picked up Abby, so when did you find the time to meet a man? I know from talking to the vet that she's a woman."

"Nan." She laughed. "If you give me a chance I'll tell you." She took a deep breath, enjoying the absolutely giddy sensation she felt. "I met him at the soccer game. He's the father of one of the boys on my team."

"Father? How old is he?" Concern knitted the woman's brow.

"Not that old. The boy in the picture with Sam is his son, Jordan."

"Well, tell me about him. I know if you're seeing him, he's single."

"Yes, he's been divorced around six years. He has custody of Jordan."

"Really." Nan's eyebrow arched up in interest. "Tall, dark and handsome."

"Tall and handsome but his hair is very light brown – sandy. You know that carpet I ordered in for Mrs. Newman? That's close. He has these intense hazel eyes, and when he smiles or laughs, he gets these crease lines that are almost dimples." She blushed at the way the woman was watching her.

"That's quite an impression for meeting a man at a soccer game." Nan kept eyeing her as if she was studying a strange new creature.

"We actually went out to lunch, and then they helped me bring Abby home. We talked while the boys played video games. Yesterday, he and his son came over, and we went swimming, then grilled steaks and watched a movie."

"So, all this was with his son there?" The apprehension was still discernible.

"Yes, except when we went to get the steaks."

"What else do you know about him?" The woman raised her hand. "It's just, you don't really have a lot of experience with guys, and I don't want you to get taken advantage of, Sweet Pea. There are a lot of untrustworthy guys out there."

"Oh, I'd say he's trustworthy. He's the chief of police."

"Chief of police! You mean Mr. Hunky that was in here on Friday?"

"Yes."

"You weren't a woof'n when you said intense. Rosebud, that man is Mr. Maleness. I heard you two going at it in here Friday. Then again, he sure did have you reacting to him. I've never seen you like that. All fire and – oh boy!" She whistled.

"Nan, don't make this more than it is. The boys wanted to hang out on Saturday. Yesterday, he wanted me to know about the picture, and we had dinner. That's all. I don't know if the rose is from him." The blush was back. Jillian looked away quickly.

"Uh huh."

Jillian could feel Nan's gaze and shifted under the weight of it.

"What else? You didn't let him kiss you?"

Jillian burst into flame.

"You didn't. You did?"

"It was just a kiss."

"Yes, but we're talking about you. I know your dating

habits. You can't call them habits, because you don't go out enough for it to be a habit. And you don't just kiss any guy you go out with. You're Miss Standoffish, my little Cactus Flower. He kissed the socks off you, didn't he?" There was a knowing expression on Nan's face and Jillian couldn't fight it.

"Nan, I've never been kissed like that before. I mean, I've never felt anything like it." She sank down in a chair as her insides turned to jelly at just the thought of the kiss.

"That must have been some kiss," the woman said in awe.

"It was, but it was more. I was already having feeling for him. It was there the first night, but I told myself it was because of what happened, and he made me feel better. But that wasn't it. It wasn't a hero thing or gratitude. I don't know. Do you think it's possible to fall in love so fast?"

"In love, oh, Sweet Pea ..." Nan took a deep breath and held it for a second before letting it slowly out. "I knew Ralph was the one the moment I met him. Though, it took a while to convince him."

"Nan, I don't know what to do. I think I've fallen in love."

"I don't know what to tell you, Buttercup, but you better think of something fast." She looked over Jillian's shoulder. Jillian turned to see Mark Richards walking toward her. He moved silently, but she couldn't figure how she hadn't heard the door, and then forgot about it as his eyes burned into her.

"Good day, ladies," he greeted them, but his attention remained fixed on Jillian. "Is there anyone else here?"

All Jillian could do was shake her head. The intensity on his face took her breath.

"Does she have an appointment right now?" he asked the question of Nan, but again his eyes never left her.

"No. She's clear for at least an hour."

"Good." He held out his hand for Jillian. She took it

without thought.

"We'll be over in that little alcove if you need us." The second they stepped into the privacy of the little nook, he turned to her. "Did you mean it?" His voice growled out like a large cat.

"What?" Jillian couldn't think, couldn't take her eyes from him. He had the fierceness of a warrior, but she knew no fear.

"Are you in love with me?"

It was her body that answered first without conscious thought, her head going up and down. Finally, the words made it out. "Yes, I'm afraid so."

"Why afraid?"

"Things like this don't happen to me. I've never been in love before. I mean really in love. I've had crushes, but I've always been just one of the guys. I ..."

"Jillian, enough said." He pulled her in his arms and kissed her. There was no need to demand a response. She couldn't have held it back if she tried. She gave herself over to the kiss. In wordless communication, he accepted her and gave of himself. They melted together, becoming one with just the touch of their lips.

One hand found its way into her silky tresses so he could angle her head to give him better access to her mouth, his other arm spread over her back, pressing her tight. Not that it was needed either. Her own arms made their way up around his neck, and she clung to him as her legs gave out.

"My Jillian." The words were whispered against her neck just below her ear. She shivered at the brush of his lips. He eased back slightly. "Last night, I thought maybe I was imagining what was happening between us. I tried to convince myself it couldn't be true. It was too fast, too much was happening. I came up with a dozen different excuses, but one thing kept denying them all. The knowledge that I'm falling in love with you."

He kissed her again, but after a minute, when she pulled back, he broke the contact.

"Mark, can this be real?"

"It has to be. It's too strong not to be."

"It's not just hormones?"

"Do you feel it is?" He turned the question back to her.

She shook her head. "No. I feel it so deep in me it's scary. I just don't know what to do."

"I think what we have to do is let it grow and strengthen. I don't want to ignore it, but we still have a lot to learn about each other." He gave her quick kiss and released her, shoving his fingers back through his hair. "This was not why I came here today." He looked back at her, longing still palpable on his face. "Okay, back under control." He took a deep breath and grinned. "How are you today?"

Jillian felt the laughter build deep within her at the absurdity of the question, working its way up and out. "Wonderful, thank you."

"You're welcome, glad to be of help. I'm feeling pretty good myself right now."

"You wanted to talk to me."

The grin slipped from his face. "Yeah, this is going to be a real mood killer." He grimaced. "I thought you'd want to know. It looks like there was an attempt on Sandra Cannon last night."

Jillian gasped. Panic hit her. "Is she all right?" She reached for his hand. He interlocked their fingers.

"Yeah. The guy didn't get close to her. We lucked out with a very observant nurse. Unfortunately, we couldn't get a description, even off the security cameras. We have an officer stationed at her room now."

"How is she?"

"They have her in a drug-induced coma. The doctors think she's going to be fine, just needs a little more time before they bring her around."

"Is she safe? Are you going to move her?"

"She's safe. We'll keep an officer on her room at all times plus the hospital security. We hadn't kept anyone posted because the psychiatrist figured he wouldn't go after her. He thought that he killed because the woman wasn't the right one."

"The right one?" A shiver ran through Jillian.

Mark shifted closer, bringing her hand to his lips. "Here, let's sit down." When they were settled, he started again. "Dr. Barlow thinks our guy is looking for his perfect love in a twisted fashion. He says it hinges on what the guy said to you – 'love me, Beauty.' He says we have a real sick monster here. Barlow said he's not going to stop until he finds his 'Beauty.'"

Shivers again washed over her. "Then what?"

Mark's countenance darkened and Jillian knew he didn't want to tell her, but he looked at her and the words came out. "Then, he'll keep her until she displeases him. He'll kill her and start again."

This time Jillian found herself squeezing Mark's hand giving him her comfort. "You'll get him."

He looked at her and she could see the pain in his eyes. "I have to, but can I get him before he kills again? If he follows his track record, we now have less than a month. Though, we have more than before, we still don't have a lot to go on. The knife had no prints. It's an upper quality knife, but it's not sold around here. It's also a couple years old, so pretty impossible to trace.

"We're still working on the mask you pulled off. It's our best lead. It's custom-made. We haven't been able to trace the maker. We do have a possibility, but the guy just happens to be in Italy, studying masks. No one seems to know when he'll be back or how to get hold of him. He's supposed to be quite odd. We have DNA off the mask so, if we can catch the guy, we'll have proof. We also got blood, thanks to Abby."

The dog appeared as if waiting to hear her name. "Hi there, girl." Mark reached out to rub the light golden fur and stroked her head. Abby laid her head on his thigh and studied him adoringly with her brown eyes.

"Abby," Jillian started to get after her.

"She's okay." Mark kept his hand on her head, rubbing behind her ears.

"You'll get hair on your pants."

"Labs don't shed much. I had a Lab when I was a kid. I should've gotten Jordan one."

"Well, you keep doing that and you'll never get rid of her."

Mark looked down at the dog then back up to her. The heat rekindled in his eyes. "That's good to know. What do I have to do to get her owner ... forever?"

Jillian's insides jumped. His expression said he was serious. She could hardly breathe at the power in his eyes. "Forever is a long time."

"I'm afraid it won't be long enough. But we might start there."

"Mark."

His name slipped out in a whisper that he caught with his mouth. He feathered the kiss over her cheek and tilted his forehead against hers. "I'm sorry, Jillian. I'm coming on too strong but I can't seem to help it, which really isn't like me." He raised his head looking down at her. "Just believe me when I say what I feel for you is love. And I think it is very rare and special. Like it was already there just waiting to be rediscovered."

"Yes." Jillian studied the man who, in five days, had found her heart.

He leaned down and kissed her quickly before shifting away. "I keep getting distracted. Back to business. Dr. Barlow still thinks there shouldn't be anything for you to worry about because the guy has obviously been picking his victims beforehand, and he still seems focused on

Sandra. Though, he is concerned that he had addressed you as he probably does his victims, with 'Beauty.' So for my peace of mind, I'll repeat. You don't go anywhere by yourself, especially late at night. No deserted clients' houses. Even with Abby, unless you've taught her to dial a phone." He waited for her to answer.

"I promise, not alone. I'll be careful."

"Good. I'll be back later this afternoon and we can go find a chime for the front door. Also, it would be good to put one on the back door, though you should leave it locked at all times."

"Nan and I already do."

"You're not going to argue with me about the chime out front?"

"As easy as you walked in here and I didn't hear you, I concede that it's needed."

"Good, though I happen to be glad there wasn't one then, or I never would've heard you say you loved me. At least for a while yet, and we both would have been driving ourselves nuts wondering what the other thought or felt. Now, that we have it out in the open, we can just enjoy and get to know each other better without all the anxiety."

"You make it sound easy."

"Something tells me it will be. This was meant to be. Now, I better let you get to work and get back myself. What time is good to install the chime?"

"My last appointment should end at three-thirty."

"Okay, I ought to be able to be here at four." He came in to give her one last swift, hard kiss. Stood, walked a couple steps and looked back. "I really like doing that." He grinned at her stunned expression. "You're real nice to kiss. Bye, Nan," he said the last loud enough to be heard in the back and strode out.

Jillian sat too stunned to move. Her finger came up to touch her lips, still tingly from Mark's. He loved her. Everything else they talked about faded away. Mark loved her. She didn't doubt him on it. She felt the truth of it, just as she felt the truth of her love for him. She sank back in the cushion of the loveseat and savored the feeling coursing through her.

Several minutes passed before Nan appeared in front of her. The woman looked bemused. "Well, I'd ask you how you are, but it's pretty obvious. Isn't that something, and when you pick them, oh, boy!"

"You're not going to warn me?"

"Oh, no, Blue Bell. I saw the look on that man's face. You've got him, and there'd be no standing in his way. I'd say you seem to be in accord so I'll just sit back and watch the show. Though, I think I'll pull out the wedding planning guide. I wondered why I kept it after Emily got married. I'll just call the caterer and see how busy they are. They were very good."

"Nan." Jillian laughed at her outrageousness. "I've known him less than a week."

"Yes. Who thought you'd fall so fast? Won't your family be surprised? Course, your mom said when you finally fell it would be hard and fast. She told me she was the same way. You'd better give them a call and give them a heads up."

"You don't think it's a little soon?"

"I don't think there is a too soon on this. I know you won't sleep with him until you're married, and with a son that age around, I don't think he'd push for that either. I also think that, now he's found you, he'll be wanting to marry soon. That man is hot when he looks at you. Well, he's hot anyway, but when he looks at you, it's amazing the air between you doesn't burst into flames."

Jillian laughed but couldn't help dream it was true. With a sigh, she sat up. "I've got to get to work."

☙❧

Mark appeared right at four. It didn't take them long to get the chime because Jillian already had an idea of what she wanted and where to get it. Nan left when they returned and at quarter after five, Mark stepped down from the ladder finished with the installation.

"How's that?" He opened the door letting her hear the tone.

"Perfect. Thank you."

"You're welcome. Now, for my fee. You owe me a dinner date."

Jillian's lips twitched. "We already have a date planned. Or did you forget?"

"I didn't forget. That was before the fact. I'm saying you owe me another."

"Oh, and am I supposed to cook for you on this one or what?"

He got a thoughtful look. "Cooking would be okay, but you don't have to. You've already made me a meal. You just have to plan what we do. Something that you like to do that we can do together." He looked around the room and frowned, "Something that doesn't involve looking at color swatches or materials."

She laughed. "I think I can come up with something. When is this to happen?"

"Well, we already have a date for Thursday. Tonight is out because I have a scout meeting to attend with Jordan, then I'm afraid I'll have to go back into work after he's in bed. Tomorrow I have city council. So let's say Friday night after your soccer practice, since I'll be seeing you Saturday already."

"You will?" She knew she sounded coy, but he just smiled going along with her.

"Yeah, you know − soccer game. Then, I figure the boys might want to hang out together again. We can do hamburgers this time. That is, if you'll have Sam?"

"I will, until two. Debbie's still trying to get it worked out so she can have the day off at least every other week."

"So, it shouldn't be hard to get the boys to want to

spend time together. I can always bribe them with a video game rental."

She laughed lightly. "That should do it for sure, but I don't have a player."

"I do. We'll just have to go to my house." He arched his brow wickedly, adding to her laughter. "Ready to go?"

"Yes."

"I'll walk you out and follow you home."

"You don't need to." Jillian cut short what she was saying and called Abby. "Come on, girl." The dog immediately stood from where she was dozing on her pillow by the desk. Jillian picked up the leash, clipped it on, reached for her purse and noticed the rose. "Can you take Abby so I can get my rose? I never thanked you for it."

"Rose?" He eyed the flower, his brows pulled together as if it disturbed him. "Jillian, I didn't give you the rose."

"Oh."

"I'm sorry, I should have brought you flowers, but things have been going so fast. I honestly didn't think of it yet. I guess I'm really out of practice with the courting thing."

"No, it's okay. I just, well, I thought it was from you because I don't know anyone else who would give me a flower," she added hurriedly.

Mark looked back at the flower. Unease settled into him. "When did you get it?"

"Nan said it was leaning against the back door when she got here this morning. That's how we got talking. She asked if I had an admirer – then you walked in." She blushed at the memory of what happened. "I just thought …"

Mark couldn't hold himself back. He stepped forward and caught her hand, bringing it up to his lips. "When I give you flowers, I will give them directly to you. There will be no doubt they're from me. And I'm thinking something bright. You know like those great big daisy things, about the size of a plate, because you have become a bright spot in my life. That is unless you prefer roses."

"No, the others are perfect. I like all flowers." A tender smile creased her lips as she gazed up at him. "I think you're pretty good at the romance thing," she whispered.

"Good." He gave her fingers a squeeze. "Let's go." He walked her out holding her hand, the flower left behind. He held her car door, catching one quick kiss before she settled in. Once in his car, he waited for her to start then followed her to her condo before turning his car toward home.

CRIEO

Jillian pushed herself in the last lap of the pool. Her muscles burned, but she felt good as she walked out of the water. Abby caught sight of her from the patio and whimpered. Unfortunately, dogs weren't allowed in the pool area.

They both missed their jogs in the park. Not that Abby was ready to jog yet, and she had promised Mark she wouldn't go there or any other place where she might be alone. Luckily, the pool always seemed to have at least a few people there in the evening making use of the hot tubs. She needed to work off some of the nervous energy building up in her.

Grabbing her towel, she wrapped it around her as she moved through the gate toward her condo. What she really longed to do was call Mark, but he might be at his meeting still, and if he was home, she didn't want to intrude on his time with Jordan. She wondered how Jordan would feel about having her around. He seemed to like her. She liked him. He was a wonderful boy. He looked so much like his father and just as adorable.

"Ready to go in?" she said Abby who danced at the end of her leash and whimpered excitedly.

"I know you want to go to the park but not tonight. Come on, I need a shower and then it's to bed."

Jillian paused at her door as a self-moving truck pulled

to a stop at the end of her building. "It looks like tomorrow's the moving day for the Greens." She waved to the man as he got out of the truck. He wasn't much older than her and had two kids, a little boy and a girl. They were such a cute family. They were able to find a small house, so the kids no longer had to share a bedroom.

Inside, Jillian locked the door and set the alarm. Turning off the lights, she headed upstairs to the shower, with Abby on her heels. Twenty minutes later, she was wrapped in a thick, soft, terry robe brushing out her hair when she heard Abby growl. The peace left her body at the sound.

"What is it, girl?" She stepped to the doorway of the bedroom. Abby stood alert at the side of the bed, her fur bristled in alarm. Instead of her attention focused at the hall or the sliding glass door, she looked up at the ceiling. "What is it?" Jillian stepped over, running her hand down the dog to ease her.

"Are you still jumpy? I've been a little that way. I'm sure glad to have you home." She stroked the Lab's head. "You're such a good girl." With a final pet, she returned to the bathroom. She just reached for her hair dryer when Abby growled again, this time from the doorway. Her attention again focused up. Jillian followed Abby's point straight up at the skylight to the face peering down at her.

The scream ripped from her.

Chapter Nine

Mark knew it was foolishness to swing by to see Jillian. She would probably think he was the obsessive type. He should go home and try to get some sleep. But Jordan was already in bed, and he just couldn't get Jillian out of his mind. He figured it was something he'd better get used to because she was never going to be far from his thoughts for the rest of his life.

He'd just stopped at the security gate to ring her condo so she could buzz him in, when someone pulled up, activating the gate. Only one parking place was occupied in front of the clubhouse, so he pulled into the closest spot to her condo and cut the engine.

The only lights on in Jillian's condo were the upstairs ones. He wavered a minute, then tugged on the door handle. He really did want to see her, and he'd only stay a minute. Okay, maybe he was becoming obsessive.

It was a nice, peaceful night. The air was warm. Maybe they could sit on the patio and talk for a few minutes. He stopped and looked again at the darkened downstairs. Maybe he should just go home and call her tomorrow. With a sigh, he started to turn.

The scream, muffled by walls and closed windows,

boomed in his heart. "Jillian!" He ran the last few steps to her condo. "Jillian!" He pounded on the door. Inside, he could hear Abby barking. "Jillian, it's Mark!" He threw his shoulder against the door in frustration, though he knew it wouldn't budge. He heard footsteps on the stairs inside. There was a fumbling at the door, and it flew open. He was through the threshold just in time to catch her as she dove for him.

He locked his arms around her, holding her tight while searching the dark room for signs of trouble. Abby appeared beside him. Mark used his foot to kick the door closed and the dog growled at it. Finding nothing amiss, he moved his hands to her cheeks, forcing her head back to look at him.

"Jillian, what happened?" He saw her fighting for control.

She managed a deep breath before she could get out the words, "A man."

"Where?" Mark's attention went to the stairs. The shrill sound of the alarm rent the air before she could answer. He released her so she could deactivate the alarm. She reached for him as she finished. "Tell me what happened."

"He was watching me." She faltered as shivers raked through her. Taking another breath, she continued. "Through the skylight."

"Skylight?"

She nodded. "My bathroom, a face staring down. Watching me. He was on the roof."

"All right, stay here. Lock the door behind me." Mark forced himself to release her. He pulled out his cell phone and hit dial while waiting to hear the lock click, before stepping out to study the building. The sight of the moving truck drew him before the voice answered. "This is Chief Richards. I need a couple of units to search for a suspected intruder." He gave the address, clicking off the phone.

Scanning the area, he moved forward cautiously, aware his gun was in its lock box in his car. A faint scraping sound was all the warning he got before the figure plowed into him.

Mark's body flew back into the bushes at the corner of the condo, softening his fall, but his head snapped back catching the side of the building. Lights flashed in his mind, blending with the sound of receding footfalls.

It was a struggle to extricate himself from the branches. He swayed slightly making it to his feet, but his police training had him turning toward the figure. For a minute, the man was illuminated in a street lamp, but dressed in black, he was still a shadow.

Mark forced himself to sprint, weaving around buildings, shrubs, and the playground equipment. Fighting to keep the figure in view, he followed mainly on instinct. Losing sight of him completely, Mark slowed. The faint squeak of a gate, followed by a click, had him shifting his direction. The small side gate led out onto the street directly across from the park. Not a soul was in sight up and down the road.

He activated the phone again, while crossing the road. "This is Richards. Relay the suspect entered the park on the north side of the complex. Don't have a visual. Suspect is a male. Approximately six feet, dark clothes." Mark kept going, meeting up with the officers searching the park from a different side.

"Nothing," one of the officers said approaching him. "I think we've lost him."

Mark nodded, knowing it was true but hating to give up on it. "Kent, why don't you have the other car keep patrolling just in case he hasn't slipped yet? You can come back with me and write up the report."

Mark started to follow the officer back to his car, then stopped and looked back over the park where a week ago a woman was almost murdered. For a beautiful place, it held a lot of ugliness lately. He didn't like it. He didn't like Jillian involved in both cases. Coincidences bothered him. Dragging his eyes away from the deep shadows, he followed the officer, anxious to get back to Jillian.

The door was thrown open before he could even ring the bell. Jillian again reached for him, though she was calmer now. He wrapped her into his arms. "It's okay," he said as he drew her close. She was soft and cuddly in a thick, white robe. It pulled at his protective instincts.

"Did you get him?" She leaned back to look up at him.

"I'm sorry," he shook his head and grimaced at the ache that settled there with a dull throb. "He got away, but they're still looking. I need you to tell us what happened."

She nodded and started to step back, her hand sliding along his collar. She froze and then shifted to his side. "You're hurt," she gasped out.

He raised his hand to the back of his head, but she caught it, pulling it away. "No. Let me see." She said, carefully moving the hair.

Mark felt a sting but said nothing.

"It doesn't look bad, but we need to clean it up. Wait here." She disappeared upstairs.

"You okay, Chief?" Kent, still standing in the doorway, asked.

"Yeah, just a bump. We'll let her take care of it while we talk."

"You know the lady?"

"Yeah, we're dating." The word seemed foreign and too plain for what was happening, but he guessed it covered it. "Why don't we get settled at the kitchen table?"

A minute later, Jillian returned and set to work tending his head while she told about Abby growling and looking up, seeing the man. "I don't know how long he'd been there. Abby only started growling about a minute or two before. I couldn't make out the face. It was all distorted. It was just the eyes looking down at me, and I screamed." Her hand trembled.

Mark reached up and caught it. "It's okay."

She nodded. "The bleeding's stopped. Do you need something for a headache?"

"I'm fine." He drew her around and down into his lap, ignoring how it would look to Kent. He needed to hold her as much for himself as for her. Almost immediately, she settled back against him, and he told his part of the story while Kent took notes. When they'd gone over it completely, the officer radioed to the other car. They had found no signs of the man.

"Jillian, I want to go out with the officer and look over the area. Just stay here and I'll be right back."

There was reluctance in her leaving his lap, but she stood, tightening her belt around her in a nervous gesture.

"I'll be just out the door." He brushed his knuckles across her cheek and placed a kiss on her forehead.

It didn't take long to figure out how the man got to her roof. It just took climbing onto the moving van to catch her balcony. Standing on her railing, the guy would just have to pull himself up on the roof, and the rain gutter happened to run down right by Jillian's balcony to make it easy.

"So, what do you think Chief? Was it planned directly at your lady, or is our guy an opportunist?"

Mark looked over where he could see Jillian standing on her patio. A fuchsia loaded with blossoms hung by her head. He wished he knew the answer. He didn't like the thought of a man right outside her bedroom window, especially while she was in the shower.

The placement of the van would have been convenient for an ambitious peeping tom. He liked that scenario a lot better than some guy out after Jillian specificity, but again, he had a lot of trouble getting past coincidences.

"I don't know," he admitted finally. "Let's treat it from both sides for now. Check if we have any other reported similar activities around here."

The man nodded.

"Could you leave a copy of everything on my desk?"

"Sure thing."

"I'll get whoever rented the truck to move it. We don't want any repeat performances." After a quick good-bye, Mark headed back to where Jillian waited. Abby was on her leash, hugging Jillian's side. He couldn't chastise her for being outside. He understood she needed to get past her fear.

"Do you know who has the moving truck?" he asked her as he approached her.

"Adam Green, two doors down." She motioned in the direction. "They're moving tomorrow."

"Okay, be right back." He disappeared for a few minutes.

Adam Green walked with him as he came back. "Are you all right, Jillian?" the man asked when he saw her.

She nodded and managed a smile. "Yes, it just scared me. I'm fine now."

"Come on, let's go in." Mark slid his arm around her, turning her to the door. Inside, he left her to get her a glass of water.

Jillian paced the room with nervous energy, Abby beside her, both golden and beautiful.

They made quite a pair, Mark thought watching them. "Here." He stepped in front of her. "Drink this."

She accepted the glass, took a drink and returned a grateful smile. "Thank you for being here."

"You're welcome." When he opened an arm, she stepped to him, laying her head on his shoulder. A shiver of pent up nerves being released shook her, and he tightened his hold.

"I'm okay now." She took a deep breath and raised her head. "I bet you didn't expect this when you stopped by tonight."

"No, but I'm glad I did." Her face showed worry,

automatically he raised a hand to wipe it away and the expression morphed to a weak smile.

"Did you need something? Is there any more information?"

"No, I was just hoping to see you for a minute." It was his turn to shift under tension. "I found myself thinking of you the whole evening. It seems that you haven't been out of my thoughts from the minute I met you."

"The minute?" She challenged, beginning to relax.

"Yes."

"Friday, you were irritated with me."

"I think I was looking for excuses to break what I was feeling. So you'd be less appealing."

"And now?"

"I like you appealing. I like the thought of you in my life."

"Mark." This time when she stepped to him, her head tilted up offering him her mouth. He took the kiss and savored it along with the feel of her in his arms. When the kiss ended, he brushed his lips against her temple.

"Why don't you go pack a bag and I'll take you to my house?"

It was Jillian's turn to pull back. "I …" Her look was one of pain and disappointment.

His brain clicked on what he said and how it must have sounded. "No, I didn't mean to my bed. You'd have your own room. I just don't want you to be here alone tonight. I have Jordan there and Mrs. Morris. You'd be safe."

Her smile was back. "I know. Sorry, I don't have a lot of experience with men. You know – tomboy – one of the guys."

"I still have a problem with that one." He grinned.

"I can use a hammer or nail gun, and do most anything any of my contractors can do." She tilted her head in a bit of a challenge.

"Oh, I don't doubt that. It's just 'one of the guys' I

have problems with. I would never mistake you as one of the guys. No guy I know has legs like yours. Have I mentioned you have great legs? I'm finding out I'm a leg man. And your hair, it's glorious. I want to run my fingers through in it. Then your eyes, they are what put me under. You have incredible eyes. I could get lost in them forever."

Those beautiful blue pools softened as they gazed up at him, and he sank into them as he lowered his mouth to hers. It was several minutes before he managed to break away from her lips to catch his breath. "You're not one of the guys, believe me. I've never wanted to kiss one of the guys like I do you. You're addicting. Why don't you run upstairs and get what you need?"

She was already shaking her head before he finished the sentence. "No, I'm not going to be chased out of my home. Please understand this. I have to stay. I can't run."

Mark started to object but before he could get it out, her hand settled on his cheek.

"It's not time yet, for me to come to you. It's too soon. Please."

He wanted to argue, but he respected what she was saying. He wanted to throw her over his shoulder and take her where he could keep her safe from the darker side of life. He wanted to be her protector. "Are you certain?"

Relief was in her smile and something more that made his heart soar. "Yes."

"Any problem, even if you just get nervous, you call me. Abby barks, you call me."

"Yes. Thank you for understanding that I have to handle this." She came up on her toes to brush her mouth over his.

He understood very well not letting fear win or control you. But it didn't make it easier. "I guess I'd better go … unless you'd like me to stay a little longer?"

"I would say yes, but you really should get home and get some sleep."

He didn't want to leave her. "I could stay on the couch."

That brought a smile. She reached up and brushed at her eye. "No, I'll be fine. Thank you."

"Have lunch with me tomorrow?"

"I thought I was making you dinner tomorrow night."

"You are. I'll take care of lunch."

"I have a meeting in the morning with one of my contractors, then a new client. I'm not sure when I'll be done."

"Just give me a call and we'll meet."

"Okay."

"Good." He gave her a quick, hard kiss and walked to the door. "Lock up after me."

ଔଅ

The door banged back against the wall. The cop had almost caught him. What had he been doing there? She was his. She was Beauty. He stared at the faces on the wall. Jillian looked back at him from dozens of different angles. Yes, she was his.

No cop was going to stand in his way. He would woo her away. He would love her and she would love him just like it was meant to be. She was his Beauty.

Chapter Ten

Jillian ran up the stairs of the police station. At least she knew where she was going this time, but she wasn't sure she felt any more comfortable. She remembered her last visit and as if she had conjured him right out of her mind, Detective Crocker appeared in front of her as she rounded the bend in the stairs. The plea that he wouldn't recognize her barely crossed her mind before he looked her up and down.

A derisive look crossed his face. "Let me guess, you're here to cry about the unfairness of life."

Jillian shifted to the other side of the step to pass him, deciding it was better just to ignore him. She was parallel to him on the step when his hand snaked out, latching onto her forearm, jerking her to a stop.

"What are you doing? Let me go." Jillian tried to pull away.

The man glared at her. "Back whining again. Such a beautiful eyeful, did you put on a good show through your peephole?"

Jillian sucked in a breath at what he was insinuating. It stung, especially after the restless night she'd had.

"I saw your name on the report," he continued. "I'm

not surprised you'd come complaining when a man looks at what's offered, and you're going to act all indignant. You've caused enough trouble. Just because you're beautiful, you think you're privileged. You're not. You'll bleed and die, just like the others."

"Crocker." Mark's voice echoed in the stairwell. "What's going on here?"

The detective glowered defiantly up. "Just came in to get something out of my desk before I go meet with the shrink." His sneer was plain to see when he looked back at her. "See you around, beautiful." He released her arm, heading down the stairs, ignoring Mark.

Jillian remained frozen on the stairs until Mark reached her. The hand he put on her arm was tender, comforting. Completely different from the one it replaced.

"Are you okay?"

The gaze he ran over her was also different from the other man's. The curve of his lips was tender, and she released a sigh of pent-up energy. "I'm fine."

Mark studied her face a moment longer until he must've been satisfied. "Good." He leaned in and kissed her forehead. "Sorry about that. I put him on leave until he completes a full psychiatric evaluation. He's not taking it well. Come on, let's get out of here." He turned her down the stairs. "What would you like for lunch? There's a pretty good Oriental restaurant down the block and an Italian across the street and a Mexican around the corner and down."

Jillian found herself relaxing. "Oriental sounds good. We're having Italian tonight, and I don't know if I'm up to spicy today."

"You okay?"

"Just nerves."

"You didn't get any rest last night. I knew I should have taken you home."

"I did fine. I've just never had things like this happen

in my life before. I tend to be pretty boring."

"Let me tell you, you're not boring."

She shook her head. "It's the new company I'm keeping. I'm the proverbial girl next door."

"Well, I find the girl next door very attractive." He looked her over.

They'd just reached the bottom step when Mark's phone rang. He looked at the number. "Sorry." He connected the call. "Richards." He listened, and then looked down at her. Jillian knew what was happening even before he said the words. There was no faking the frustration in his voice when he said, "All right, I'll be there in twenty minutes."

"I know," she said as he disconnected. "You've got to go."

"I'm sorry. The mayor wants a meeting now. He's getting a lot of pressure from the press. There's a conference scheduled for one-thirty."

"I understand."

"This really doesn't happen often. I want you to know that I won't break dates often."

"I said I understand, and I do. It's all right." She could tell it really bothered him and that made her feel warm inside.

"I'll swing by and see you after the conference and take you home."

"You don't need to do that. I'll be fine. I'm being very careful."

"I'll still try to be there. I'll call you later."

Jillian decided to take control of the situation and gave him a kiss. "Get going. I'll see you later."

⊗

Mark came around to open Jillian's door then went to get Abby from the back. As promised, he appeared at her studio just before closing to pick her up, and no amount of persuasion could dissuade him from driving her home, even pointing out that he'd have to drive her to work in the morning.

"I still can't believe you've never played soccer." Jillian continued the conversation that had been going on during the drive.

"What can I say?" He shrugged. "It was football and baseball in my school. I was into football and also ran track."

"Really, which events?"

"Hurdles, two hundred and four hundred."

"Now, I am impressed."

"I didn't say if I was any good."

"It doesn't matter. I can't imagine doing hurdles. I tried once. I tended to jump them. You know, like regular jump. The time I did come close to doing it right, I caught the hurdle and went down. That ended it for me. And though I was quick on the soccer field, I wasn't nearly fast enough for a sprinter." She looked over at him. "So were you any good?"

"I placed third in state on four hundred, fourth on two. So fair, just not spectacular."

"I'd say that was spectacular. What did you play in football? Wait a minute, let me guess. The quarterback, calling the plays."

"Nope, tight end, I was fast, could jump and good hands to shift into a receiver."

Her next comment failed to come out as her, "oh," changed to a gasp as a man popped up from behind the railing of her patio.

"Hi, Jillian. These are for you."

Abby growled faintly as she, too, was startled. Jillian sagged against Mark's arm.

Mark shifted back from the defense move he made to shield her when he recognized the man. "Toby," he said sternly. "You can't wait and pop up like that. You scare people. It frightened Jillian."

Toby's look turned to one of concern. "I'm sorry." He looked to Mark and back to Jillian. "I didn't mean to frighten you. I wanted to give you the flowers." He shoved the large bouquet of long-stemmed, red roses toward her.

Jillian swallowed. Getting herself back into control, she stepped forward and took them. "Thank you, Toby." She lowered her nose to draw in the fragrance. "They're beautiful. Why are you giving me flowers?"

"You're supposed to give a girl flowers when you like her. Roses. Red roses."

"Oh," Jillian wasn't sure what else to say. "Thank you."

Toby looked at Mark. "Have you given her flowers before?" It was said as a challenge.

"No, I haven't," Mark replied.

Toby looked satisfied at the answer.

"Roses smell good. Do you like them, Jillian?"

"Yes, Toby, they smell nice and are very beautiful, but you shouldn't have spent your money on them for me."

The boy-man shifted. "They are American Beauties. I know 'cause Sandra got some." That comment made both Jillian and Mark freeze.

"You gave Sandra American Beauty Roses?" Jillian asked the question before Mark could.

Toby shifted again uneasily, and Mark repeated the question. "Toby, did you give Sandra American Beauty Roses?"

"No. She got them from a secret admirer, right after she got her picture in the paper. She was excited." He looked at the flowers in Jillian's hand and glanced down. This time it was Mark's question that caused her pause.

"Toby, did you buy these flowers for Jillian?"

He weaved from side to side.

"Toby?" Jillian pressed.

"I wanted to give you the flowers." Toby kept his eyes on the ground.

"I understand, and that was very nice of you, but where did you get them?"

He peeked up at her like a child caught with his hand in the cookie jar, which Jillian thought was a fitting analogy. "They were by the door."

Jillian knew instinctively that the words were coming, but still had to fight to keep from dropping the flowers. Her breath caught. Beside her, she felt Mark tighten.

"They were here when you got here?" Mark asked casually, but Jillian heard the tension in his voice.

Toby nodded still looking down. Jillian stepped forward placing a hand on his arm. "It's okay Toby, I'm still glad you gave them to me."

He looked up at her. "I wanted you to have flowers. Guys give flowers when they take a girl on a date. Will you go on a date with me?"

Jillian smiled gently, though her insides quaked. "I can't. I'm dating Mark. I don't date more than one man at a time."

Toby sent a glare at Mark. "Will you date me when you stop dating him?" He shifted from side to side.

"We'll have to wait and see Toby. I like Mark a lot. I'd like to date him for a long time."

"Are you going to marry him?"

Jillian felt herself blush. "I might, it's still soon, but I love him already."

Toby kicked his foot on the ground.

Jillian squeezed down the hand she had on his arm. "I'm sorry, Toby. I didn't mean to hurt you."

He pulled back from her.

"Toby," Mark drew his attention to him. "Are you certain Sandra got roses like these?"

For a minute, it looked like Toby wasn't going to answer, then he nodded. "She told me all about them. She'd never got roses like them before. She didn't know who gave them to her, but she was real excited. Jillian, will you still be my friend even if you marry him?" He looked pleadingly at her, and then sent another glare at Mark. "I knew you first."

"Of course. I'll always be your friend," she assured him, patting his arm.

He nodded and looked up. "I brought Abby another bone." And he pointed to the bag on the patio table.

"Thank you, Toby."

"If you want flowers, I'll bring you flowers. They sell them at work."

"That's not necessary. But, thank you. I'm just glad you're my friend, and Abby really loves the bones. Toby, we have to do something now. So I have to go. Bye." She shifted, anxious to talk to Mark about what Toby said.

"Okay, Bye."

"Just a minute." Mark stopped him as he started to turn. "Toby, one more question? Did you see who left the flowers?"

Toby shook his head.

"All right, thanks, Toby."

The man sauntered away, glancing back several times at Jillian. When he went around the corner of the clubhouse Mark saw him duck back behind the bushes so he could watch them. "Come on, let's go in."

The minute they entered the apartment, Jillian dropped the flowers as if they were poison ivy and turned to him. "There's a connection between the roses and The Beast."

Though she voiced his thoughts, Mark didn't want her going too far with the hypothesis yet. "We don't know that."

She eyed him. "But you're thinking it."

She was too bright, or she knew him too well for the short period of time they had been together. "I'm wondering. We don't know for sure. Toby's information might not be very reliable."

Jillian stared at him for a minute then went to her desk,

found a piece of paper and dialed the number. "Mr. Cannon? Hi, this is Jillian Taylor. Yes, I'm fine. How is Sandra tonight?" She listened and smiled. "That's good. I heard about that. No, she's great, getting around with no problem, but we're still not jogging yet. Mr. Cannon, what I called you for was to ask a question. I'm really sorry to bother you about this, but did Sandra receive any flowers lately?"

Her face clouded as she listened, and her voice shook on the next words. "Yes. They are. Would you mind if Police Chief Richards and I went and got them? We don't know. He was with me when someone mentioned that she received roses and we wondered. I agree, they'll keep her safe, and they're doing all they can. They'll get him. Try not to worry about that. Yes, I'll call later. Thank you. You, too. Bye."

She hung up the phone and turned to him. "Sandra received a dozen long-stemmed, red roses about a week before the attack. Her father said he thought they were probably still sitting in her room if you'd like to look at them. We can go now and get them. Her brother should be home."

It didn't take Mark long to make up his mind. "Let's go."

The wilted roses were still there, draped over the vase on her dresser. They looked like they would have been similar to Jillian's when fresh, and like Jillian's, there wasn't a card. Sandra's brother confirmed that because he'd teased her about it.

"You're troubled," Jillian observed as he secured the dead flowers in the back of his car.

"I'm afraid I'm about to ruin the rest of our evening. I'm not going to get dinner with you. I'd like to go over to Tina Kimball's apartment. She was the victim before Sandra. Her apartment's is still empty. Though it wasn't the crime scene, the family wasn't ready to go through it yet and agreed to leave it until the rent was up just in case it might help." Mark didn't want to leave her, and relief filled him at her question.

"Can I go with you?"

Mark didn't need to debate. "Are you sure you want to go?"

She nodded. "Please."

"All right. We can stop for something to eat when we're done."

ෆ෩

They had no problem getting the landlord to let them into Tina Kimball's apartment, but it was obvious that the man wasn't anxious to stick around. After fidgeting a minute in the hallway, he left them alone on the promise that they would lock up and return the key to him.

Jillian couldn't blame the man. The pleasantly decorated room of sage green and rose gave off a tomb-like feel. A light layer of dust had accumulated on everything. Jillian had to fight the urge to throw open the windows and let in fresh air.

Mark moved through the living room as if noticing nothing amiss. Jillian shivered, feeling foolish. She had worked in old, abandoned places quite often, but there was something about knowing that the person who lived here had died a violent death that, even though it hadn't happen here, lingered.

They split, Mark going into the bedroom while Jillian moved into the kitchen. It was easy to see there were no roses there, but a tall, crystal vase sitting beside the sink caught her attention. It didn't take much imagination to see it filled with the fragrant blood-red blossoms. She was freaking herself out. Still, she drew closer to examine the vase visually, knowing better than to touch it. A dried leaf stuck a couple inches below the lip.

As a designer, she had taken a botany class for her science credit so she had no trouble identifying it as a rose leaf. Though she had no way of telling what color the roses were or how long the leaf had been there. Again, it wasn't hard for her imagination to pull up the image of a grieving family member tossing the wilted blooms away when they cleaned the perishable foods from the fridge, then leaving the vase by the sink.

Turning around, she spied the wastebasket by the fridge. It was empty, even the liner was gone. Still, Jillian moved closer to investigate. There on the floor between the wall and the fridge were several dried, shriveled, blackened petals. Her fingers trembled as she picked one up. Even age didn't completely hide that it had once been red. Her stomach felt like a lead weight settled in it, and her legs went weak. She put a hand on the fridge to steady herself.

Tina had received flowers just like Sandra had – like she had. No, it couldn't be. The thought ran through her, and she shook her head in denial as the truth of it sank in. It couldn't be. It was just coincidence.

Jillian fought to get breath back in her lungs and hold off a wave of sickness that threatened. She lifted her eyes, letting them roam over the room before her gaze was drawn inexplicably back to the fridge. She froze. The woman in the newspaper clipping stuck to the fridge wasn't familiar, through the caption told her all she needed: 'Tina Kimball awarded the Top Realtor of the Month.'

"Jillian."

She jumped at the sound of Mark calling her and turned just as he came into the kitchen. "Nothing in the bedroom. What is it?" He was at her side before she could begin to form words. One arm slid around her, pulling her to his side as the other came up to cradle her face. "What is it, sweetheart?"

She raised her palm, holding the petal to him. She saw the significance register on his face.

His eyes immediately started to search the room. "Where'd you find it?"

"On the floor, by the waste basket." She pointed, "And Mark." She pointed at the fridge. His gaze followed to the clipping. She felt him stiffen and knew he'd made the same connection as she did.

♞⍺

"Come on, let's go." He took her hand, wanting to get her out of there as fast as he could.

They rode in silence. If either thought of food, neither said so. Finally, Jillian spoke up. "Where are you taking me?"

"My house." He couldn't get his mind off the possibilities of a connection.

"Mark, I can't." When he didn't budge, she continued, "What about Abby?"

"We'll pick her up." He flipped on his turn signal.

"Mark." There was objection in the sound of his name.

He wasn't surprised by it. "Look, I know it might be nothing, but I'm not willing to risk it or risk you."

She was silent a minute then reached out to lay her hand on his arm. "Pull over, please."

Mark went another couple hundred feet before he complied. He sat, staring straight ahead, hands locked on the wheel, afraid that, if he looked at her, he would crumble to her will.

"Look at me, please." When he didn't, her hand came over to pry his fingers from the steering wheel. There was a shifting beside him, and a second later, she dropped over the console into his lap.

He tried to close his eyes, but it was no good. The second her lips touched his, they flew open, and he took another dive into her deep blue pools. The warmth of her lapped over him, and he was drowning in her. A smile played at the edge of her lips, and a hand came up to caress his face.

"I appreciate you wanting to protect me."

He started to speak, but the hand shifted to lay a finger

on his lips, keeping the words back. "I know what you're doing, and it's wonderful, but it's too soon. We don't know for certain that there's a connection. We don't know if the flowers are from the same guy. We don't know if he knows me, if −" she swallowed. "If I'm a target."

"Jillian." The finger couldn't keep her name from slipping out.

"I know. I won't say I'm not frightened." There was a tremor in her voice, and his hands clamped around her. "Could it be that he knows who I am, that he's now turned to me?" Her eyes searched him for the answer.

Mark fought the urged to yell out in frustration. "I don't know, but I don't like the possibility." He tightened his hold.

Jillian tipped her head down to rest against him. She only rested there a second before easing back. She studied his face. "I don't like the possibility, either, but I can't go home with you. It's too soon. Jordan doesn't know anything that's happened. He hasn't had time to even start accepting me. How would it look if he woke up and I was there?"

"Jordan actually likes you already. He told me that on the way home last Sunday. He was wondering if I was going to date you."

"He did?" A twinkle picked up in her eyes before she turned back, looking serious. "Still, I can't come home with you. We're rushing things as it is, especially for me, Mark, I can count all the men I have ever gone out with on two hands, ones that I have let kiss me on one. I have never let a man kiss me like you do, and I've known you a very short time.

"I take it that means you've never sat in any other guy's lap." Mark felt his own lips pulling up. His hands spanned her back, running up and down. Her intake of breath was gratifying, as was the shiver that ran through her that he knew had nothing to do with fear or tension. It was all heated awareness, and it blazed in her eyes.

"No." She tried to rise but he held her there.

"You started this. Finish it."

She raised her chin defiantly. "I won't go home with you."

"If I don't concede right now, what else will you do to persuade me?"

She looked at him shocked and then relaxed. "How about a kiss as reward for agreeing with me?"

"I didn't say I agreed, but I do concede I might have overreacted and rushed things. You're right. We are moving fast, but that doesn't worry me. I know how I feel and it couldn't be fast enough for me. I do need to talk to Jordan some, but I can't have you in danger. This guy is a psycho. He's a killer. And the moment I find that he is after you for certain, you are going to my house, a safe house, or I will lock you up if I have to, whatever it takes." There was no give in his voice. "No argument on that."

She was slow to nod but did. "You'd lock me up?"

"Yes. In the most secure cell I have, if that's what it takes. But, until we find out one way or another, I will take you to work and pick you up. If I can't make it, I'll have an officer do it. You will check ID before you go with anyone, as a precaution. I'll pay someone to watch the shop for you so Nan can go with you or I can pay someone to accompany you – whichever you like. You're not to be alone, ever."

"I have ball practice tomorrow night."

"I'll take you if I can. I'll also try to stay. If not, you'll be with the kids until I get there to pick you and Jordan up. Agreed?"

"Yes."

"You're not going to argue?"

"No, I know what this guy did – will do, if it's him. I'm not stupid. I hate it in movies, when you know the bad guy is waiting outside the door, and the woman walks out to see if anyone is there. I'll be careful."

"Good." Mark knew he sounded stern and didn't expect it when her lips twitched again.

"That brings up one thing." Her voice dropped to teasing. "I never checked your badge to see if you're you."

His mood jumped to meet hers. "Considering you're sitting on me and I can't get to it, I guess I'll have to prove it another way." He swooped in, not giving her any time to pull away. Not that she tried. The kiss was all encompassing. He savored it, savored her. She was his.

"Oh wow, you have quite a way to end an argument."

"We may have to argue a lot. And, I think we need to make it a rule that you sit on my lap when we do."

Jillian laughed. "That did work out pretty well. I wanted to get your attention."

"You got it, but it would probably be best if you climbed back to your own seat now."

Chapter Eleven

Mark's mind drifted from the play on the soccer field. There was nothing concrete. They still had no link to the flowers, though Sandra and Jillian's were the same variety, they didn't know yet about Tina's. They also didn't know if the other victim had received any roses. If she had, she didn't mention it to anyone who could remember for certain.

One thing they did come up with was that her picture did appear in the newspaper within a month before her murder. She was on the board for a local fundraiser and had been interviewed regarding it.

All three, four including Jillian, had their pictures in the paper. All sounded like they were good people. Jillian and Lori served the community, Tina was a hard worker and conscientious person and Sandra's quick reaction saved a child. They were all beautiful, within five years of the same age, and they all were fair haired, blondes to light brown.

Too many similarities. It had to be a pattern – a pattern Jillian fit. Mark figured that, if he wanted to try to be positive about it, if Jillian was the next victim, then it gave them one up on catching the killer, knowing where he was going to strike. It didn't make him feel better.

He watched Jillian go after the ball as the boys tried to pass to keep it away from her. She was Monster in the Middle. He laughed as she almost slipped and went down, but at the last moment, she got a toe on the ball, deflecting it out of the circle. The passer traded her spots, and the game continued.

His gaze went to his son. Jordan loved soccer, and Mark was beginning to understand why. It was a lot of fun. He was catching on pretty well, for an old man without any experience. The boys had to work hard to take the ball from him when he joined in the practice. He'd have to get Jillian to give him some one-on-one practice. She'd already promised Jordan that she would help him.

He smiled at his son. It looked like things were going perfectly between him and Jillian. Jordan thought she was great, and she seemed to return the sentiment.

The ball came his way, and Mark managed to make the pass. His mind only stayed on the drill only a second before it shifted to the discussion he'd had with Dr. Barlow. The doctor advised caution. He went over the conversation.

"If the killer found out Miss Taylor's identity, he could shift to her," Dr. Barlow had speculated.

"Why would he do that?"

"It could be for several different reasons. She took his victim away, threw off his rhythm. He had it all planned, was executing the killing how he liked, but Miss Taylor interrupted that. So he wants revenge or maybe something more in another area all together."

"Like what?"

"It's hard to say. A lot could depend on how much he's hooked on his routine. It could be because she does fits the profile he's looking for, and she was able to prevent him. He might see her as better than the rest; that maybe she is the one. Or it could be as simple as she is the next in line. This man has a ritual. If the flowers are from him, they could be part of it. The pictures in the paper may be how he finds them, but they have to have certain qualifications. The thing is, his time line seems to be off if Miss Taylor is next. He has usually waited about a month between them. I'd say he takes the time to pick his next victim. He has accelerated that, maybe because Miss Taylor fit perfectly and was right there. I'd say he's becoming more volatile. What is certain is that he's smart and dangerous."

Mark was jerked back to the present as the ball came his way. He moved to get it but was too late and the boy snuck it away. Amidst rolling cheers, he took his place as the Monster in the Middle. A minute later, Jillian blew her whistle and split the boys up for a scrimmage. By the time they were finished, Mark felt he'd had a good workout.

"How about we take Jillian home for dinner?" Mark asked Jordan as he helped the boys gather up cones.

"Sure, but she might be a little tough." Jordan quipped then laughed at his own joke.

Mark tossed a ball at his son, which Jordan dodged and chased after, still hooting with laughter.

It was Jordan who took over, asking Jillian to dinner on the way to the car. "Dad wants you to come to dinner. Are you going to come?"

Jillian looked surprised. "Is it okay?"

"Yeah. We can watch a movie after, if it's not a mushy one. I don't have any homework."

"Actually, I'm not much of a mushy movie fan. I like action and adventure."

Mark saw the man loitering by the car just before Jordan said, "Hi, Toby."

"Toby, I didn't see you there." Jillian started in surprise. "Why didn't you come over to practice?"

"You didn't need me. He was there."

Mark caught the man's glare.

"Mark's going to help me when he can. You can still help." Jillian stepped toward Toby, but the man pulled back.

Toby's eyes went to Mark then back to Jillian, softening as they did. "He might not like me hanging around if you're dating him."

"Toby, I'm still your friend. I told you that already. If you want to come to practice, you can, all right?" She waited until he nodded. "Good, we're all done for today so I'll see you later. Okay?"

He nodded again and ambled off with his hands shoved deep in his pockets.

Mark watched him go before turning back to her. "You might want to be careful around him."

Jillian looked up surprised. "Toby? He wouldn't hurt a fly."

"I'm just advising caution. He still has a man's body, and a man's hormones, even if his mind and maturity level is behind." Mark wasn't sure what he was warning her about for certain, but he just wanted her to be careful.

"He's very conscious of his strength. He tries hard to please people."

"I understand." Mark wanted to press it but was worried he was coming off over protective. Luckily, Jillian's next words took the need away.

"I'll be careful."

"Thank you." He leaned down, gave her a peck on the cheek, then looked over at Jordan, who'd been watching them in silence and winked.

Jordan grinned back, seeming to accept what was happening between him and Jillian.

 CBEO

Mark brought his cereal bowl and juice to the table and sat next to his son. "So what's on for tonight?"

"Nothing. Are you going to see Jillian tonight?"

"Possibly. Is that okay?" Mark decided it was as good a time as any to talk about it with him.

"Yeah, I like Jillian."

"So you said the other day, but I was wondering if it's all right with you, if things got serious between us."

Jordan thought for a minute. "Yeah, it's okay. Are you and Jillian dating? I mean I know you went out, but are you going steady?"

"Well, I don't think I'd use the term going steady but, yes, things are becoming serious with Jillian. I care for her a lot. It's been a long time since I've cared for a woman like I do her. I need to know how you feel about that. It affects you, too. I won't do anything that, well, you can't handle."

"I like Jillian. She's fun, pretty, and she's nice."

"Yes, she is."

"Dad, is Jillian in danger?"

Mark froze at the question. "What makes you ask that?"

"I get it that you like Jillian a lot. But there's something bothering you, too. You're worried about her."

Mark shook his head. Jordan was growing up too fast. He was also very observant. "You're right. I am worried. Do you know how I met Jillian?"

It was Jordan's turn to shake his head but it was in the negative.

"There's a killer who's been attacking women. Jillian was jogging with Abby when there was an attack on a woman. Abby saved her."

"That's when Abby got hurt?"

"Yes. Well, there's a possibility that the killer has found out who Jillian is and is after her. We don't know yet. Until we do, I'm trying to keep an eye on her when I can, and Jillian is being careful not to be alone."

"Why doesn't she just come and stay here?"

Mark liked how his son thought. "Jillian feels it's too soon yet. She was worried what you'd think. She doesn't want you to feel that she's going to interfere with our relationship. Which she won't, but she wants you to like her."

"I do like her. I think she should come live here."

"I'll talk to her about it."

"Are you going to ask her to marry you?"

Mark hesitated only slightly, deciding to get it all out. "I'm thinking of it. Would you be okay with that?"

There was a thoughtfulness that came over Jordan then he nodded. "I think you should get married again, and I think Jillian would make a good mom."

Mark wasn't too surprised at Jordan's directness. He always pretty much said what he thought. They'd set a rule long ago to be honest with each other.

"I'm thinking she would, too. We'd better get you to school. Come on."

♋

It was funny Jillian thought, as she watched the boys gather up their gear and head for the cars. She missed having Mark at practice tonight. Even though he'd only been there the one time. He'd seemed to fit. Warmth flowed over her. He seemed to fit in every part of her life. She tried to convince herself that it was too soon but there was no way to deny that she was in love with Mark.

She wanted to burst with the sensation just as she wanted to burst when Jordan had greeted her at practice with a hug around her waist. What ten-year-old boys still gave hugs? She smiled, hers did. She turned to watch him, and then had to look away. He was her boy. The strength of the feeling had her brushing away a tear.

A movement she caught out of the corner of her eye had her jerking back around. Jillian didn't quite know what attracted her attention, but she searched the area toward the baseball diamonds, playground and the concession building. She wanted to dismiss it, but the ice that seeped through the warmth she was feeling wouldn't let her.

Someone was there. Then she saw the flash of sunlight off a lens. She wished she could believe it was the sun reflecting off a plain piece of glass or metal, but she knew it wasn't. She could almost hear the camera shutter whirl. There was no doubt he was taking pictures of her!

She froze then shook it off. No, she was being paranoid, everything was getting to her. She caught the motion of whoever it was pulling back and knew it wasn't paranoia.

The hoot of victory was loud enough to catch her attention. She glanced to the side, unwilling to fully look away. The quick action was enough to spear her with fear. The other boys were gone. The parking lot was completely empty. The park was deserted, just Sam and Jordan remained.

Terror spiked as she watched the boys run over toward where she'd seen the flash. Balls scattered all over the field, the closest not more than twenty-five feet from the concession booth. She knew the yelling was Sam and Jordan seeing who could kick the farthest.

"Sam, Jordan, come back!"

The boys slowed.

"We'll get them," Sam yelled back, and the boys raced again.

Jillian didn't even realize she was running until the first ball flew high over her head back toward the ball bags. "Jordan!" she cried out. "Sam!"

The boys had already passed where she'd seen the flash. She scanned the area and saw nothing. He was gone. Please, let him be gone. The words ran through her mind just before she caught sight of him. He was still there, back farther in the shadows, by the bleachers, between them and the parking lot.

Jillian's stride faltered, as she became caught in his sight, like invisible threads wrapping around her. It was him. It was The Beast. She could almost hear him say 'Beauty' in her mind as he reached out a hand toward her. She shook her head.

His hand made a slashing motion then both arms stretched out beckoning her to him. She wanted to scream, but the breath froze in her. Unconsciously, she took a couple steps back away. His attention shifted to the boys.

It was enough to break the spell that bound her. "No!" she yelled at the Beast. "Sam, Jordan!" She ran for them. No way would he get close to the boys.

The boys must've heard her distress, because they froze and turned toward her. Jillian reached Jordan first, and wrapped her arm around him. Sam took a step toward them. Jillian caught and pulled him into the circle of her arms while looking back over her shoulder. She'd lost sight of The Beast.

"Jillian, what's wrong?" Jordan stood straight, and though his head only came to her shoulder, he was alert, scanning the area much the way she had. Proving he was his father's son, he was ready to protect.

Jillian looked back to where the man had been, but he wasn't there. Again, she wanted to believe he was gone but didn't dare. "We need to get back to my bag. My cell phone is there." Her voice hushed. She couldn't keep her fear from seeping out. "Just leave the balls and let's stay together."

"Dad should be here soon," Jordan added by way of assurance.

Jillian pleaded that it would be so. She searched the area again and saw nothing.

"I don't see anything." Jordan echoed her words.

"Me, either," Sam added. "What you looking for?"

"Nothing." Jillian forced a smile to her face. "I just spooked myself that's all." She wanted the words to be true, but she still couldn't shake the feeling.

He was still there, watching, waiting.

     ⊰⊱

He wanted her. She was right there. She was perfect, the one. She had even known he was there. She was linked to him, but she wouldn't come to him. Why wouldn't she come to him? It was those boys. They had drawn her away. They had kept her from him. Well, he could wait. It wouldn't be long now. After all, the time had to be right. If it was too easy, then she wouldn't be worth it.

He watched the SUV pull into the parking lot and raised the camera. The high-powered lens focused in on the man getting out, and he snapped a picture. The cop was really beginning to annoy him. The oh-so Mr. Everything Police Chief. He knew the type. He'd dealt with them all his life.

In school, they were the teacher's favorites, wore the cool clothes, and had good homes. He was the type whose mom would've baked cookies for him, not called him a beast. In college, he would have been popular. Girls would've flocked around him, and he would've had his pick.

Well, it was different now. It was his turn to on be top. He'd have his pick. And the cop couldn't do anything to stop him. Mr. Police Chief didn't know anything. None of them did. They would never get him, and soon, very soon, he would have Beauty.

CB&EO

Mark pulled into the parking lot. He was late. Frustration rolled through him. It wasn't hard to find Jillian and Jordan. Besides Sam, they were the only ones there. They were coming toward him, and some of his frustration faded at the sight of Jillian's arm around Jordan. They were fitting together almost better than he could have hoped for. Life wasn't too bad.

"Hi." He slid out of the car. "Sorry, I'm late. Traffic accident happened right in front of me. I had to stay and help until the units could take over. How was practice?" The trio was close enough now that he could see the tightness in Jillian and concern in his son. Something had happened. His long stride cut away the distance between them. "What happened?" He reached the group, opening his arms to encompass them all.

"Something frightened Jillian." Jordan was the first to answer, and Mark locked his attention on her. She was already shaking her head.

"It was nothing. I just scared myself. Someone was watching the practice and I let it scare me."

"Where?" Ice shot through him.

"It was nothing, really. With everything ... I let my imagination run away with me." She tried to brush it off, but he could still hear the stress in her voice.

"Where?" he repeated. She shifted under the weight of his eyes. It was a skill he'd cultivated, and it served him well with criminals and reluctant witness alike. It didn't fail him with Jillian.

"Over by the concession booth, but it was nothing, really. There was just a man there. He was back in the shadows, and he was taking pictures. I thought he motioned to me. It spooked me. It's foolish. I'm a little tense. I've never been dropped off to a soccer practice before by a police car." She forced a smile on the end.

"I thought it was cool." Sam spoke up.

Mark sent the boy a smile. "Good, I'll tell you what. How about you boys gather up the rest of the balls and gear, while Jillian and I take a walk over there? He could see the objection starting to form in Jillian, but she kept it down. The boys took off. He took her hand, interlocking their fingers and steered her toward the building.

"Where'd you see him?"

"Mark, this is silly. Now that time's passed, I think I really did just scare myself. I feel so embarrassed that I acted that way around the boys."

"When did you see him?"

She sighed, giving into the fact that he wasn't going to let it drop. "At the end of practice. I was thinking how much I missed having you with us. I realized everyone else was gone. Then I saw him. He was kind of hidden. It looked like he was taking pictures, and I thought the camera was directed at me. That's all it took. When I saw how close Jordan and Sam were to where he was, I freaked."

"What did you feel?" When she hesitated, he gave her hand a squeeze.

"That he was watching me." Her breathing picked up. "He reached out a hand like he was beckoning me. It was eerie, terrifying."

Mark slid his arm around her, pulling her close. They walked around the area but saw nothing. He had Jillian go over everything in more detail. Finally, he gave up and returned to the boys, but he decided next practice he'd have some surveillance on hand.

Four hours later, Jillian relaxed back in Mark's arms. The movie was a good one, but she was more interested in the man who held her. His heartbeat was a soothing sound. His chest was firm but not too hard. It made a great pillow. She snuggled against it, taking in a deep breath of his scent. She liked his musky smell. It was so him, not overpowering but nice, sexy. She rubbed her head on his chest again.

"Are you going to fall asleep on me?" His voice rumbled from within him.

"No, this is just very nice."

"Agreed." His hands caressed her back.

"You ought to move Jordan up to bed." She looked down at the boy stretched out on the floor. Abby was pressed alongside him. They were both asleep. It really did look like she was losing her dog to the boy.

"I think you may have competition for your dog's affection."

"Yes." For some reason it didn't surprise her that his words followed her own thoughts. They seemed to be very in-tune to each other.

"I should've gotten him a dog a couple years ago.

Don't know why I didn't. You come with bonuses."

"Bonuses?" She turned in his arms, lifting her head to look up at him. "As in plural?"

"Oh yeah." He tightened his arms, pulling her to him. "As in plural."

The words were whispered against her mouth before his lips settled down. Pleasure rushed through her at the taste of him. She wrapped her arms around him and gave herself over to the kiss. One hand came up to burrow into her hair, tilting her head while he feasted on her.

When his lips lifted, all she could think was "Oh, wow," and it slipped out.

He smiled down. "Yeah, that is one amazing bonus. You're a pretty sweet package."

"You're pretty good yourself." She reached up and ran a finger across his lips. "I hate to crush the moment, but you really ought to take Jordan up to bed and then take me home."

A serious look crossed his face. "Why don't you spend the night here?"

"Mark." She pulled back. "I'm sorry, I can't."

"Again, I'm not talking about sleeping with me. I understand it won't happen until we're married, and I agree with that. I'm talking about your safety. I'd like you to stay here." His shoulder tensed under her hands. The hand on her back tightened, but this time not to ease her to him.

Jillian felt his onslaught coming and hurried to cut it off. "This is about what happened at practice, and I told you I just let my imagination get the better of me."

"I'm not certain about that. You're a smart woman and observant. You recognize patterns. Though, you tend to look at it from an artistic side, it's still the same. Something bothered you. It wasn't right and you noticed it. I'm not going to dismiss it, and I don't want you to either."

"Okay, but I'd still like to go home. The other day you said the psychologist said he followed a pattern, and it's usually been a month between victims. Well, it's only been barely over two weeks."

"Closer to three. He also warned that things were off. It could be that he has accelerated his routine. This guy's violent and he's unstable."

She studied the man she'd come to love in just a few short weeks. He was becoming easier to read. "What else have you found out in the last few days?"

The hesitation was easy to see but with a sigh, he continued. "We traced down the man that made the mask. He just got back into the country. He couldn't tell us much. It was ordered online. The address it was shipped to was a rental. We're looking into the name of the person it was rented to, and the police there are helping us."

"And?" She knew there was more.

"There are two unsolved murders that fit close enough that it looks like the same guy."

Fear edged in that even Mark's arms couldn't hold back. She lowered her head to his chest and felt his lips brush her head. Her mind worked over the thoughts coursing through her. When it stumbled over something, she pushed back to look at him. "Is there more?"

He looked grim. "I guess it won't hurt for you to know this," he said after a minute. "The mask was from what the maker called his fairy tale collection. It was his Beast from Beauty and the Beast."

Her breath caught. "And he called me Beauty."

"Yes."

"And a rose is part of the story, if I remember right."

"Yes. I picked up a couple copies, and though it's different in each story, a rose always has a part, as does a magic mirror, and the fact that the beast needs Beauty to love him to break the curse plaguing him."

She lowered her head back to his chest. His arms tightened around her again, but this time it was a hug of comfort. Once more, his heartbeat sounded in her ears. The rush of feeling was deeper and maybe even more meaningful.

"Where do the newspaper articles come in?" She broke the silence.

His lips brushed her head again. "I don't know. It could be just how he finds them. It could be more. We're still looking. We have been able to confirm that other victims did have their photos in the newspaper shortly before their deaths, one about two months before she was killed, the second a little over a month. So it does fit." Frustration rang in his voice.

Jillian sat up slightly over him, looking down at him. "Hey, you'll get him."

"Will I? I don't know. What if he takes off again? Then it starts all over again someplace else. What if I don't get him, and he comes after you?" His anguish was heart wrenching.

"Then you'd better get there and save me."

"I'd rather we didn't get to that point."

"I agree, but I still need to go home."

Several seconds passed until his chest rose and lowered with a large sigh. "All right, I'll take you home. But−," he held up a finger, "you get scared again, or even if you just change your mind, you call, and I'll come get you."

"Agreed." She couldn't keep the promise from him.

တဢ

"Nan, I'll be in the car," Jillian called out, grabbing up her purse, and hefted the storage tote, stacked with design layouts, samples, and other things she wanted to go over with the contractor she was heading to meet. Jillian felt relaxed and happy, more than she'd been for two weeks. The weekend had passed problem-free. She'd spent the whole time with Mark and Jordan. Her team had won their soccer game again. After lunch and errands, they had gone back to her condo, spent the rest of the day at the pool and the evening watching movies.

Sunday they picked her up for breakfast which they made together at his house. They hiked up to a waterfall just out of town and had a picnic. It had been a great weekend.

She smiled as she juggled the tote while unlocking the trunk. Clouds had moved in overnight that weren't showing any sign of burning off, but they didn't dull her mood. She loaded everything in the trunk while Nan locked the door. Jillian hummed as she went to the driver's side door, unlocked it and slid in.

The music froze in her throat as her eyes came up to the rear view mirror.

Chapter Twelve

Beauty

The word scrawled in red across the rear view mirror ripped into her, shattering her contentment. Jillian spun in the seat, afraid he would be there, behind her in the back seat. It was empty. She sank back weakly. The scream erupted from her when the passenger door was pulled open.

"Heavens, Sweet Pea, what was that for?" Nan dropped into the seat, her hand going to her heart.

Jillian couldn't get the words past her pounding chest. Her gaze went to the mirror and Nan's followed.

"Oh, my!" the woman gasped and pulled out her cell phone. Her conversation was lost in the ringing in Jillian's head.

It was the killer.

She wanted to deny it, had been trying to, but it was impossible now. He did know who she was and he really was after her. She wanted to cry. She wanted to scream. She had finally found love, and this psycho was there to put a shadow on it.

She hadn't registered Nan getting out or coming around the car until she touched her elbow. "Come on, let's get you inside. Mark will be here in a couple of minutes."

Jillian forced a deep breath into her lungs, stood and nodded. "I'm all right now." It was a lie, she knew. She was shaken to her core, but she could handle it. "Will you call Ryan and let him know we'll be at least an hour late meeting him? Have him just get started on the bathroom. There are no changes there. He can put the scaffolding up in the entry. It's set to go. We'll go over the kitchen when we get there."

"Sure, just let me get you a cup of tea first, something to calm you down." Nan's arm was around her, as if afraid she was going to faint.

Jillian found herself able to smile at the image of Nan trying to hold her up if she did. "I'm fine. I'm not going to fall apart." But that was what she did, nine minutes later when Mark walked through the door. His arms opened just in time to catch her as she launched herself to him.

"It's okay. I've got you," he murmured against her neck, burying his face into her hair.

His muscles were tense under her hands. His arms, like steel bands, locked around her. She was safe. She held tight to his body several minutes before she eased back. "I'm okay, but I'm glad you're here." The smile she gave him was watery. His hands came up to frame her face. He kissed the tears away.

CR80

Mark didn't ever want to let her go. There was no denying it now. He'd felt fear like he'd never known when he'd saw the mirror. He pressed his lips to the side of her head taking in the scent of her. There was a touch of berry under the subtle smell of her perfume. He loved that smell, just as he loved the feel of her in his arms. Unfortunately, there were things that needed to be done. One thing was for sure, he was not leaving her on her own again.

"Tell me what happened?"

"There's nothing to tell. Nan and I were going to meet with one of my contractors. I got in the car, looked at the mirror. I don't know how long it had been there. I hadn't been in it since you followed me to work this morning. We just picked up lunch at the deli around the corner. I had a client here that took up most the morning, then I worked on some renderings."

The trembling in her body increased as she talked. Mark drew her close and started to rub his hand up and down her back. She went lax against him, her head resting on his shoulder. She didn't keep it there long enough to suit him, but it was her statement that jarred him when she lifted her head, bringing it all to bear.

"He's watching me. I'm next."

Again, he caught her face between his hands. "He's not going to get you." He forced her to look at him. Searching for a way to get her to understand just how important the promise was to him – how important she was to him.

"I love you. I'll keep you safe. Do you understand that? I won't let him get that close to you." He opened his soul to let the truthfulness of his words glow into his eyes as he took his fill looking at her. "I love you, Jillian, love you like I've never imagined. It would rip me apart to lose you now that I've found you. I can't, won't let that happen."

"Mark." She raised her hand to his cheek, cupping it. He shifted a hand to cover hers and press it there to soak up the love that came through her touch.

His eyes didn't leave hers. "I've been lonely for so long." He let out what he had never even acknowledged aloud to himself. "When I married Jordan's mother I was looking for someone to fill that loneliness, but she was never the one. Since then, I've used work and Jordan to fill my life, and it's been enough. But, I've still known I was missing something. The night I met you, I knew what I was missing – you. At first, I was afraid to admit it, afraid to hope, afraid if I did, it would be snatched away. I can't let this psycho take you from me."

"Mark." Was all she seemed to be able to manage, but it was all that was needed. Her love was so clear for him to see. It matched what he felt bursting from him. Her next words echoed the words in his mind. "I love you."

"Good. Because I want to spend the rest of my life loving you." Again, he framed her face with his hands. "Jillian, please, marry me?"

"Yes." The word seemed to slip out, like there was no way to keep it back, like she didn't need to think about it. It was right. Just as it was within him, in every part of him, that she was the one he was waiting for. He was the man she loved and would forever. Her mouth was already on the way to his when his lips caught hers.

Intense pleasure and joy wrapped around them, pushing away all the darkness that lurked outside, and they knew only each other and their own world of love. When the kiss ended, they sat contented in each other's arms. One of Mark's arms was wrapped around her shoulder, as his hand brushed caressing strokes over her cheek.

The little chime that he had installed on the back door sounded, and they both pulled back. "I keep picking the least romantic spots and times that I can."

She gave a little laugh, hugged him tight, and then looked up. "I don't feel like anything is missing."

"Oh, really." His heart soared. The panic he felt from Nan's call forgotten. "We just got engaged in the middle of your shop, in the middle of the day, and I don't even have a ring for you. I think a lot of women would say I made a huge hash out of it."

"I'm not like a lot of ladies."

"You got that right. You're one of a kind, very special." He kissed her again, quick and hard.

"Chief Richards," Nan stepped up behind them. "One of your men would like to speak to you out back." There was a grin on the woman's face that said she enjoyed the whole show.

Mark looked down at Jillian, feeling the tightness slip back into her body. "I'll be right back." He placed a kiss on the end of her nose before he headed to the door. "Major hash," he muttered to himself, but Nan must have picked it up.

"On the contrary." The woman brushed at moisture on her cheek. "I thought it was nicely done." Nan stepped by him to Jillian. "Well, Rosebud, you sure caught that man."

Jillian's eyes came up and met his, and he felt the heat of them. It was all he could do not to go back and take her in his arms. He should be able to do that. After all, they just got engaged. The moment called for them to be together, instead, he forced himself out the back door to the menace waiting there.

∽∂∽

"I'm engaged." Pleasure ricocheted through Jillian's body. "I'm going to marry Mark. I can't believe it. It's so soon, but it's right. Nan, I know it's right."

When the woman chuckled, Jillian joined in with laughter of her own. She felt wonderful. "I'm marrying Mark."

"Yes. Oh my blossom, isn't it something? I told you I needed to pull out my wedding planning book. Men like him don't want to wait when their mind is made up."

"Oh, what about Jordan?" A fissure of unease slipped into Jillian. "How will he take this? It's so sudden."

"I'd bet Mark has already talked to him, Sweet Pea. And what's the problem? I thought you and Jordan got along great."

"We do. He's a wonderful boy. But that was me dating his dad. This is me being his new mom. What will he think of me as that?"

"Any child would be fortunate to have you as a mom. Now, quit worrying."

Jillian laughed again, letting the happiness wash over her. "You're right." As she stood, a little of the reality of life slipped back in. With her deep breath, she took a step to the door. "I'd better go see what's going on. I don't think I finished answering questions."

"You two got a little distracted."

Warmth came back into her at just the thought of getting engaged to Mark. Jillian wrapped the thought around her like a shield as she stepped out the door.

Mark was beside her car talking to an officer whom she recognized from the night of the attack. He was a detective. There was another man scrunched down leaning into her car.

She only took a couple steps toward them when the figure appeared in front of her. The flash blinded her, and Jillian stumbled back. Her foot came down on the edge of the back step and slipped off. A scream caught in her throat as pain spiked up her ankle. Her hands scraped over the side of the planter, but she managed to keep her head from striking it. Still, she impacted with the ground with enough force to knock the breath from her lungs.

ᏅᎤᏅ

Mark jerked around at the small shriek in time to see Jillian fall. He knocked the man aside in his dive to catch her, but he was too late. "Jillian!" He came down beside where she sat awkwardly on the ground by the stoop. "Are you okay, sweetheart?" He reached for her head first, lifting her chin.

She nodded, took a couple deep breaths. "Yes. Just got the air knocked out of me." Mark gladly caught her up in his arms, but when he eased her up, and she placed her foot down, she winced.

"What is it? You're hurt."

"I think I twisted my ankle." She leaned into him and lowered her foot tenderly to the ground. After a couple of tries, she let it take her weight and sighed. "It's okay."

Mark kept his arm around her.

At the faint whirl of the camera, Jillian jerked and

turned. Mark shifted positions to shield her, glaring when he recognized Clark. "What are you doing here, Clark?" He snapped, not bothering to hide his annoyance. He wanted to send his fist into the face of man whose action had caused Jillian to fall.

"What is it? Is it the killer? Did he strike again? Did he attack Miss Taylor?"

"No. Why are you here?" Mark released Jillian, taking a step toward the reporter. "Are you stalking Miss Taylor?"

"Hey, back off. I'm just doing my job. I heard the address on the scanner with a request of a forensic unit." The reporter lifted a hand in front of him as if it would help ward Mark off. He backed up a couple steps as Mark kept coming.

"And how did you know it was her address?"

"I'm a reporter. I'm supposed to know. Besides, it wasn't hard."

"Yeah, but to memorize the address so you knew it as soon as you heard it?" The challenge was clear. Mark wasn't sure what he was getting at.

"That's what it takes to be a good reporter."

"Harassing someone?"

"I'm not harassing anyone."

"Wrong, you're harassing me and my fiancée. You caused her to fall, possibly causing injury."

"Fiancée?" The reporter locked on the word.

"Yes. We're engaged. And I don't like you following her around distressing her." Mark glared the man down even though they were close to the same height. "I want you to stay away from her. You understand? I don't want to see you around her again, or you'll be facing charges."

"You can't do that." There was a whine in the man's voice.

"Wanna bet?"

"You can't do that. Freedom of the press," he stressed like it was a shield he wielded.

"Don't even try to go there. You stay away from her." Mark turned his back, cutting the man off. He slid his arm around Jillian, directing her back inside the door. He seethed with pent-up energy. It was all he could do not to hit the man, but he didn't realize how taunt he was strung until Jillian's hand brushed his cheek and slid down the side of his neck to rest on his shoulder.

The instant she stretched up to press her mouth to his, his anger morphed into passion. His arms locked around her pulling her into him. He pressed her back against the door. The groan that escaped her only seemed to fuel him on. He needed her, craved her. The shiver he felt cruise through her body was in answer to the one that ran through his.

It was the sound of the telephone that finally pulled him back to reality. He broke abruptly, panting as he tried to get air back in his lungs. Jillian looked so dazed and wanting, he almost crumpled back into her, but he straightened himself and eased away.

"I am not going to make love to you the first time in your shop," he growled out more to himself, but Jillian looked up in shock. Her expression told him she wanted him every bit as much as he wanted her. He felt the laughter rise in him. His mood changed once again. "Oh, you are a pleasure. I can't wait to get married." He took another deep breath. "Are you okay?"

"Yes!"

"I meant your ankle."

"Uh, oh, yes. It's just a little tender."

"I'm going to have to do something about Clark," he said it under his breath, but as close as Jillian was, she heard and answered.

"I have to admit, he gives me the creeps."

"Has he bothered you at other times?"

"No," Jillian was quick to answer, and he could tell there was more she wasn't saying. All he had to do was wait and it came. "I've seen him a couple times. He was outside the shop the other day watching from across the street. I thought he followed me, but when I looked back again, he was gone. I saw him another time when I came out of the store. I'd stopped to talk to Toby who was getting carts. He was sitting in a car, watching again." A shudder ran through her.

"What is it?"

"Nothing, I just thought how he was taking pictures. Maybe it was him who was at the soccer practice. I thought the man was taking pictures. It might have been him."

The tentacles of unease ran over Mark as she said the words, making him slow to respond to her next question.

"Why is he so interested in me?"

"He thinks you can lead him to a story on the killer." Venom dripped from Mark's voice.

"You think he set me up by putting the picture in the paper? But how could he know that was how the killer finds his victims?"

"He probably didn't – doesn't. We're not sure about that, and we haven't released it. I think he put your picture there just like dangling a carrot in front of a horse to get his attention. And it looks like he got it. Now he's hanging back to see what story he can build. I'd guess he's working you into a front page deal, and I just added to the pot letting him know we're engaged."

She nodded. "I can see the headlines. Police Chief's Fiancée – Serial Killer's Next Victim."

"I'm not going to let that happen."

"I know, but I think the reporter's going to play it up."

Mark didn't want to admit he thought so, too. "I'll have another talk with him and warn him off following you."

"Will it help?" There was doubt in her eyes.

"Probably not," he admitted.

"Who would have thought that I'd have to worry about

the paparazzi?" she said lightly, bringing a smile to his lips.

"Now, I think we'd better call your parents and let them know you're engaged just in case it does make the papers." He took her hand, giving her fingers a squeeze. "Where were you heading when you went out to the car?"

"Oh, I need to meet with one of my contactors."

He was amazed that even after all the things that had happened to her, she could show such excitement at the thought of a job she was working on.

"Okay, after we talk to your parents. I'll drive you." He could see her objection coming then she dropped it.

"Are you sure you don't mind?"

"Never."

"It's up on Station Hill, the old Van Buren mansion. I can't believe I get to do the restoration. This could really set me up as a designer. I mean, I'm doing well, especially being relatively new, but this is so high profile. I'm very fortunate to have been chosen. Sharon Van Buren actually saw something I did for Elsinore Reed and contacted me. The house is fascinating. It has all these odd rooms, and there are actually secret passages. She is going to turn it into a museum. I've been able to locate some great wallpaper and tapestry for the curtains."

Mark nearly laughed at how animated she had become, talking about the house. When she paused to take a breath, she looked at him and blushed. "Sorry, I didn't mean to go on like that."

"Don't worry about it. I can't wait to see it."

"Well, it doesn't look like much right now. It's sat vacant for about thirty years, ever since the timber mill closed and her brother died. It's going to be terrific when it's finished. The contractor doing the restoration is fabulous. He only handles restoration work. I feel very lucky to work with him."

"Should I be getting jealous about now?"

"You have nothing to be jealous about. Ryan's good-looking and talented, but I don't love him." She looked thoughtful for a second. "I don't know why, but he doesn't appeal to me. He's a great guy. I guess he reminds me too much of my brothers, whom I still need to introduce you to. Anyway, the connection just wasn't there like it is with you." She smiled brightly at him. "You were it the moment I met you."

Mark thought about pointing out that the moment she met him, she had just survived an attack from a psycho and was scared to death, but decided against it, because he knew what she meant. She was right for him from the start.

"Let's make a phone call." He held out his hand.

CRBO

The old house was much as he expected, monstrous and grand at the same time. Neglect hung heavy on it, but he could see the possibilities as Jillian talked.

Ryan Stoddard was also close to what he had imagined, and if he hadn't been so sure of Jillian's love for him, he might have been jealous. The man would be considered very good-looking to women with his sandy hair and tanned skin. The man had his own six-two height by a couple inches, and his body was tempered strong from years of construction work. Intelligence blazed in the man's blue eyes. Mark liked him from the moment they shook hands.

After a quick tour of the house, including a jaunt through the maze of secret passages, he stood back and listened while Ryan and Jillian discussed the restoration and the next steps to take on it. They were finished and about to head out to the car when the contractor asked if Mark could help him support one of the scaffolding pieces, while he secured it.

"Sure." Mark agreed then turned back to Jillian as she spoke.

"I'm going to take these to the car."

"I don't …"

She cut him off. "I'm just going outside. I'll be right back. I'll even leave the door open if it'll make you feel better."

He wanted to protest, but it sounded foolish. When he looked back at the contractor after watching Jillian walk out, it was obvious Ryan agreed.

"There've been some threats against her." Mark felt the need to explain as he helped hoist up the two-inch diameter metal tubing.

"You're kidding." The man froze. "Who'd want to hurt her?"

"A very sick individual who's already killed several women."

"You can't be serious. The guy I've read about in the paper? He's after Jillian?"

"It's possible."

"Wow, so that's why you're with her. I mean, beside the fact that you're engaged."

"Yeah. Listen, I'd appreciate it if you could make sure she's never alone here, even with Nan. I know Jillian thinks Nan is enough, but I don't think so."

"You got it. I'll make sure I'm always here before she gets here and leave after she does."

"Thanks, I appreciate it," Mark said as the man tightened down the cross piece. Mark reached for another section just as a scream pierced the air.

Chapter Thirteen

Jillian set the tote in the back of the SUV, smiling at Mark's silliness. Like something could happen to her twenty feet from the front door, but his concern was so sweet. She closed the tail gate and turned just as a man burst from the bushes. She was stumbling back before she recognized him, but by then, it was too late. Gravity and mud on cobblestones took control of her body, and she went down.

The cry ripped from her lungs as she hit the ground.

"You're going to marry him!" Toby yelled at her, eyes wild, tears flowed down his face. "No!" he shouted at her then repeated it as Mark burst through the door, followed by Ryan. Toby looked at her, the anguish in his face shifting to fear.

"Toby." Jillian recovered enough to get his name out, but it was too late to get him to listen to reason.

"No." It was a whimper this time, and he took off, sprinting across the massive overgrown lawn. She watched helplessly as he disappeared.

"Stay with Jillian," Mark ordered Ryan as he sped past.

It was Jillian's turn to yell. "No!" But it did no good.

Mark was in full pursuit mode, though Toby had a

huge head start on him. Mark cleared a three-foot-high shrub at the edge of the drive in perfect hurdler's form. "Mark!" She tried to call him back as Ryan skidded to a stop beside her, almost going down himself.

"Are you all right?" He knelt beside her.

"Yes, I just slipped."

"Don't worry, he'll get him. Are you okay for me to help you up, or should I get an ambulance?"

"No. I'm fine. You need to go after Mark."

"I'm sure he can handle him." There was no doubt Ryan was trying to soothe her, but he wasn't getting it.

"No, it was just Toby. He wasn't trying to hurt me. He just startled me. We have to get Mark back. He frightened him." She looked toward where the men had disappeared. "We've got to go after them." She started to rise.

Ryan caught her hand to help her up.

The pain in her ankle was more pronounced than it had been earlier, and she almost went down when she touched her foot to the ground. There was no stopping the gasp of pain that escaped her. "Twice in one day," she ground out, fighting back the tears that threatened to fill her eyes.

"You'd better stay still." Ryan tried to lower her back to the ground.

"No, it's just my ankle. I twisted it a little. Please, I need you to go after Mark to stop him. He's frightening Toby."

"I can't leave you," the man said firmly. "Let me help you sit down."

"I'm fine. Please help Mark." Her plea ended as she caught sight of Mark coming through the trees marching the dejected form of Toby in front of him, controlled by hands cuffed behind his back.

Jillian broke away from Ryan and hobbled toward them as they approached. "Mark, no." She reached for the frightened young man.

"Jillian, stay back."

"No, Mark why did you cuff Toby?"

"He attacked you and took a swing at me."

"He didn't attack me. He startled me, and I fell. And you frightened him." In the distance, she heard the sound of a siren and groaned. "Mark, he didn't attack me, please."

"Jillian, he's following you. You can't argue that. He came after you."

"He was upset. He must've overheard us talking about being engaged." At her words, Toby made a heart-wrenching mewing sound and dropped to the ground.

"Toby." Jillian stepped toward him, ignoring Mark's scowl. "Toby, I'm sorry. I would've come to tell you."

He jerked back when she moved to lay her hand on his shoulder.

"Toby, there wasn't time to tell you yet. We just got engaged today."

The man was rocking back and forth, sobs racking his body.

"Can't you release him?" She looked up at Mark who shook his head.

"Toby, why did you try to hit Mark?" Tears flooded her eyes as the police car pulled up. "Please, Toby, won't you talk to me?" She felt lost. Pain jabbed in her at the forlornness of the boy-man.

Behind her she heard Mark talking to the officer, and the man came to take Toby to his cruiser. "No!" Jillian tried to object, but Mark's arm locked around her, holding her back. He turned her, and Jillian went weak as tears swamped her. "No, please." She pleaded into his chest. "He's frightened. Don't you see he's frightened?"

Mark was at loss what to do. Jillian's words and pain ate at him, but he couldn't release the man. No matter what Jillian thought, he'd been following her, and he had attacked her.

More disturbing, though he hadn't told Jillian, Toby knew not one but two of the other victims for certain. And though he didn't want to believe it, he had to take him in for questioning. He fit the height, and he had taken more than a couple of swings at him. His side throbbed from the contact, but it didn't hurt as much as the tears of the woman he loved, and was afraid he was losing.

The groan almost ripped free. This couldn't be happening. They had only been engaged a couple hours and now this. It should have been one of the most beautiful days in their lives. He tightened his hold, afraid she would slip away. Her words deepened the feeling when she pulled back.

"I want to go with Toby."

"Jillian, I can't let you do that."

"You really don't think Toby could've killed those women do you?"

He wished he could give her the answer she wanted, because he really didn't want to believe it, but he wasn't going to take the chance, not with Jillian's life on the line.

A howl split the air when the officer tried to ease Toby into the cruiser. He went wild, thrashing back and forth.

"Toby!" Jillian broke free, rushing toward him. Mark caught her hand, and she spun to face him. "Let me go."

The anger in her eyes froze him. He lost his grip.

She hobbled her way to the car, getting between Toby and the officer. "Toby!" she yelled, gripping his shoulders. She almost fell as he spun. Instead she wrapped her arms around him and held tight. "Toby, you have to calm down," she pleaded. "You have to calm down. Shh," she continued when a wail broke free. "It's okay. It'll be okay, but you have to calm down. All right? You're making this bad. Please, Toby." She stroked his head, and he dropped it her shoulder.

Her body bowed at the weight of holding him up, but Mark didn't dare step to her. Whether in fear that he'd incite Toby again or Jillian would shun him, he didn't know. Her voice had dropped to a soothing level as the man cried on her shoulder. She rocked him like she would a hurt child, which in some ways was what Toby was. It was evident when Toby lifted his head like a chastened child and sobbed.

"I'm sorry, Jillian." He sniffled. "I shouldn't have hit Mark."

She wiped the tears from his face. "No, you shouldn't have."

"I didn't mean to hurt him. I didn't mean to make you fall." He cried harder.

"I know. It's okay."

"You're mad at me."

"No, I'm not mad at you. But, you have to be good. You have to go with the officer. Okay?" She waited, and he finally nodded. "They will call your mom. Okay?" He nodded again, and she forced a smile. "Look at how exciting. You get to ride in a police car." She injected brightness in her tone, and the smile spread to Toby, then he looked over her shoulder to Mark.

"Do I have to apologize to him now?" He looked abashed.

"You probably should, but if you want to wait until later that would probably be all right. I know he scared you."

"He chased me because he was mad."

"Yes, he thought you hurt me."

"I'm sorry. I was mad at you."

"I know. I'm sorry your feelings were hurt. Will you go with the officer now?"

He nodded, and got in the car.

Jillian turned to the officer. "Please, he didn't mean to cause problems."

"I'll handle him with more care, talk to him about what's happening."

"Thank you." The smile she gave the man was warm. Mark wondered what her expression would be when she turned back to him. Would he be as easily forgiven?

The officer looked over to him and nodded.

Mark nodded back, but his attention stayed fixed on Jillian, who didn't turn to look at him. The officer got in the car and drove off. Jillian stared after them, her arms clamped in front of her.

Mark started toward her, aware that Ryan had disappeared. He stopped a step behind her, unsure how he would be received.

He couldn't take it any longer. "Jillian," he groaned out. To his astonishment, she turned into him, wrapping her arms around his waist, pressing her face to his chest. Mark was more than happy to return the hug. The fear that gripped his heart slackened. He still didn't dare move, afraid to break whatever spell had her in his arms, but the words slipped out. "I was so afraid you were angry at me."

"I am." Her hand fisted and smacked his chest then ran up to circle around his neck, pulling him even tighter as she cried with deep sobs. "I feel like something is trying to tear us apart. I wish it would all end."

"I'm so sorry. I wish I could make it all go away." He pressed a kiss on the top of her head, helpless to do anything else but hold her and pray he wouldn't lose her. Several minutes passed before her crying stopped. When her hand came down to wipe her cheek, he eased her back. "Jillian?"

The voice came up but her head didn't rise. "How could you arrest him?"

This time, his groan made it out. He placed a finger under her chin and tilted her head up. The sadness in her eyes did him in.

"I'm sorry. I know you're used to befriending him, but Toby keeps popping up in our investigation. He's a person of interest. If I go with my instincts, I'd say he's not involved, but the evidence continues pointing to him and I can't ignore that. Everything needs to be checked out and investigated thoroughly."

Tears again filled her eyes.

They ate at him.

"But," she shook her head in protest, "you can't."

"I'm sorry, sweetheart. I have to. Please don't be mad at me."

"I can't help that." She raised her hand, wiping away tears from her cheek. "Just like I can't help loving you. It's just not easy right now."

Mark grimaced. At least she said she loved him, though the other didn't bode well. He decided to try for the positive. "Let me take you home. Your pants are muddy and wet. You've been through a lot of turmoil – your emotions have been ricocheting up and down."

"I should go to the station with Toby until his mother can get there."

"I don't think that would be a good idea." He knew he was already weakening. "I'll tell you what. We'll pick up Abby at your shop, then I'll drop you both at my place. Jordan can keep you company, and I'll go down and check on Toby. If you stay there, I promise not to press charges unless we turn up some hard evidence and need to hold him. Will you agree to that?"

She was quiet a moment then her shoulders dropped in defeat, though Mark felt like he was the one who lost.

He felt more lost four hours later when he walked back into his house. He moved quietly toward the family room where he heard a movie running. The two people he loved most in the world were watching the screen.

Jillian was stretched out on the couch. Jordan lay on the floor with Abby pressed along his side. Mark's heart would have soared if it hadn't been so heavy. He knew his news was going to crush Jillian. As if sensing his presence, she looked back over her shoulder, stood, and came to him.

ଓଃଠ

Jillian didn't need to touch Mark to feel the tension in

him. Something was wrong. Her head started to shake in denial, but his pain pulled her forward. She wrapped her arms around him and held tight until some of his stiffness eased.

"What is it?" She brushed her hand across his cheek, intrigued by the rough texture against her finger tip.

He caught her fingers and brought them to his lips.

"Mark?" The unease soared in her as she met his eyes.

He led her into the kitchen, released her hand to pace the floor a couple times before coming back to stand in front of her. "We found Toby's car parked down the block from the mansion."

He gritted his teeth, and she started to shake her head before the words even finished their way out.

"Inside there were several pictures of you. There was also a copy of Beauty and the Beast."

"No." She couldn't keep the cry in.

"Yes. He's been following you. It was him there at the soccer practice that scared you."

"No!" She didn't want to believe it, couldn't believe it.

"Yes, the picture was there. You with Jordan and Sam, others of you going into your apartment, out by the pool, at the store."

"But still—"

"No, Jillian. There's more I'm not at liberty to discuss. I'm so sorry."

"It can't be him." She cried, frantic in her fight to right her world. "It can't be Toby. I pulled the mask off. The guy's head was bald. It wasn't Toby, it wasn't."

Mark wrapped his arms around her. She wanted to fight and cling to him at the same time. Clinging won. She pressed her face into his chest, unable to keep tears back. "It wasn't him. I felt the rough skin on his head."

"Maybe what you felt was his cheek. The scar he has there. You were frightened and it was dark." He tried to reason as his hands moved up and down her back in an effort to soothe her.

"No," she whispered one last denial, going limp against him. She was relieved that he didn't try to stop her tears but held her as she cried. She was drained of all energy when the flood finally ended. Her eyes felt too heavy to keep them open, she closed them, and she gave herself over to him to hold up.

"Come on, you need to get some sleep. It'll be better in the morning." He brushed his lips against her temple.

"Why do people say that?" She managed to raise her head and open her eyes to look at him.

"Probably because they don't know what else to say to make it better." He brushed his lips to hers. She nodded, moving with him as he turned. Instead of stopping to collect Abby next to his sleeping son, he kept going toward the stairs.

"Where are we going?" Her brain was too sluggish to wrap around where he was leading her.

"I'm going to take you upstairs, find you something to sleep in. While you change, I'll come down and get Jordan and tuck him in. If he heard that, he would say he's too old," Mark said trying to add a touch of lightness. "Then I'll come back and tuck you in. You may have to fight my son for your dog."

"I can't sleep here." She blinked to clear the sleepy, muddled feeling from her mind.

He turned to face her straight on, placing a hand under her chin to tilt her face up to look at him. "Yes, you can and you will. Don't worry, I'll control myself. In fact, I will be across the hall. I want you awake and your full attention on me when we make love for the first time. Tonight, I wouldn't get either of those things. You're worn out. Your emotions have been tossed all over the place today and you're still torn up about Toby. So don't argue. You shouldn't be alone tonight."

The kiss he gave her wasn't filled with passion but it

was enough to blow the last of the circuit she still had functioning in her brain.

She was hardly aware of him leading her up the stairs. She was in the center of a room before it registered it had to be his. "This is your room?" She turned to study it, even her sluggish mind could take in the details.

It was a wonderful room that fit him very well. The bed was beautifully carved wood. She knew he had picked it out himself. It fit him so nicely and looked so comfortable, she wanted to curl up in and be surrounded by it.

"Yes." His answer finally registered. He opened a drawer of a tall dresser and pulled out a pair of old, worn sweat pants. "These will drown you but will have to do." He opened another drawer and took out a T-shirt.

"You picked your bed."

"Yes. You don't like it?"

"I love it. It's beautiful." She ran a finger over it and almost giggled at the surprised look on his face. She must be getting punchy.

"High praise from the designer. How do you think the painting you have over your fireplace will look hanging over it?

She squinted, trying to picture it and shook her head. "No, it'd be better on the wall over there."

He followed her finger and nodded. "We'll have to check it out, but, not now. My designer needs to get some sleep." Again, he guided her, but this time it was across the hall and down several doors. "The bathroom is there. You can sleep here." He opened the bedroom door." Get changed and I'll be back in a minute to check on you."

It'd taken him five minutes to get Jordan settled in bed. Abby once again was stretched out beside his son with Jordan's arm draped over her. Mark smiled. It looked like Jordan was getting a dog. Closing the door behind him, he crossed the hall to the guest room. At the sight of the woman standing in the middle of the room, his heart crumbled.

Jillian stood statue stiff, looking utterly lost. His sweat pants and shirt bagged on her. She looked adorable and forlorn at the same time. She didn't hear him push open the door or step up behind her.

"Oh, sweetheart," he whispered, wrapping his arms around her. She jumped slightly then went weak against him.

"I don't know what to do." Her voice was hushed. She turned to him. "I can't believe that it's Toby – that he could kill those women. Mark, it's so impossible."

"Try not to worry about it." He brushed the hair back from her cheek.

"I can't help it. I keep seeing him huddled in a cell."

"I should have told you. We moved him over to the psychiatric ward at the hospital for evaluation. He's not in a cell." He didn't add that part of the reason he pushed so hard for it tonight was for her benefit almost as much as knowing Toby couldn't handle being in the cell. His heart jumped at the look of relief Jillian gave him.

"Thank you." She leaned into him.

He gratefully accepted the hug, running his hands up and down her back. When he felt the shiver of released tension quake her body, he eased back. "Let's get you to bed. You need some rest."

"It seems like you keep trying to get me into bed." An impish look crossed her face, and he couldn't hold back the groan.

He met it with honesty. "You shouldn't tease a man who wants you as much as I do and has been celibate as long as I have. I'm trying to be honorable here."

"Mark." This time it was her that brushed a hand over his cheek. "I'm sorry, I didn't realize. So much has happened today. It was just that today we got engaged." She looked stunned at the realization. "It feels like we've been together forever."

He understood what she was experiencing. It was the same for him. It seemed weird to even think of life before her, and he couldn't imagine it without her. "I know. A lot has happened lately, but would you mind making this a really short engagement? I want the wedding to be nice," he added hurriedly, "but, is a couple months possible?"

"I'd say it's a definite possibility, especially if I set my mom and Nan on it. How about we pick out a date in the morning, and get them working on it?"

"I'm for that." He kissed her hard this time letting passion seep through.

"Umm. That was very nicely done."

"What was?" He tried to look innocent.

"Distracting me." She smiled. "I feel better now."

"Good, climb into bed and I'll tuck you in. I'm afraid you've lost Abby to Jordan. She's curled up beside him."

"I make her sleep on the floor at home," she said pointedly as she slid under the covers.

"Well, it's only for one night."

The look she gave him said 'yeah, right'.

He laughed. "So maybe both the Richards men will get sleeping companions out of this wedding." He leaned in to kiss her. She was so beautiful. Her golden hair was fanned out on the pillow around her head. The haunted look that had been in her eyes was now gone, though the drowsy appeal remained.

He brought the blanket to her chin, not that it did anything to hide her allure. He couldn't keep from running his fingers over her cheek. Her skin was so soft. A smile crested her lips, and more than anything he wanted to slide in beside her.

"How's your ankle?" He tried to think of a safe subject.

"Better. Just a touch tender. Are you going to sit with me until I go to sleep?"

"I thought I might, since my son has your dog."

"Oh, I see. I guess that's only fair."

"You said Abby wasn't allowed in your bed. Does that mean I have to lie on the floor?"

"You said she was in bed with him."

"Lying right beside him, his arm wrapped around her."

"Then I guess it would only be fair." That was all the encouragement Mark needed. He stretched out beside her on top of the covers and pulled her to him. Her arm came out to drape over his chest, and she sighed next to him.

"Go to sleep." His voice came out a husky growl, but she just smiled and complied.

Chapter Fourteen

He was there. She could feel him over her. Light glinted off the knife as it descended. "Love me, Beauty." The haunting words snaked out of the darkness. "No!" She screamed, fighting back at the grotesque features. She dug her fingers in, wanting to free herself from the demon. She felt rough skin and tried to pull back.

"Love me, Beauty." The voice came again demanding that she comply.

"No!" she cried. "No, I love Mark." Her mind caught on the name and formed a picture of the man who held her heart. She clung to it and used it to pull her free of the nightmare.

◌◦◌

Light filtered in around the curtain, giving a faint illumination to the room. There was nothing threatening in the unfamiliar surroundings as Mark's scent helped wipe away the dredges of the dream. Mark – a smile made its way to her lips canceling the last tendrils of fear. She pictured him the night before tucking her in bed, lying beside her, his arm draped over her, sheltering her.

The thought of sleeping beside him the rest of her life brought a rush of excitement. They were going to set the date this morning. He said he wanted the wedding as soon as possible. Well, she could agree with that.

Stretching, she pushed back the blanket. There was no sign of anyone in the hall when she peeked out. She almost laughed at the image of herself in the mirror. Her hair was a wild mess, and her shape was almost obliterated by Mark's clothes. Happily, she wrapped her arms around herself.

Back in her room, she looked at her clothes draped over the chair. A sound out the window caught her attention before she could start to change. She pushed back the curtain and blinked as the sun blinded her for a moment. She had to blink again as a tear rushed into her eyes at the sight below of the boy and dog playing in the backyard.

Jordan and Abby raced across the grass together. Abby no longer showed the effects of the attack. She bounced off as Jordan flipped a tennis ball high into the air. Tears threatened to slip free as she realized that it wasn't only her dog, but her son, enjoying their time together.

She was so wrapped up in the sight that she didn't hear the man come up behind her, but she didn't jump when his arms circled her. His lips on her neck did bring a shiver of awareness though. He worked his way up to her cheek. When he came in contact with the moisture, he froze, his arms tightening.

"Are you all right?"

Jillian nodded then swallowed so she could get the words out. "Look at them," was all she could manage to reply.

She felt his body relax. "They're having a great time." His lips returned to nibble against her neck.

"I have a son." She sniffled. Again, his arms tightened around her, but it was in a hug.

"I take it you don't mind that." His words were thick with emotions.

Again, she felt too choked up to get words out so she

just shook her head.

Mark turned her in his arms and, with one hand cupped her face, tilting it up to him. "I love you." His head dipped, and she was rewarded with a kiss that sent her heart soaring higher. When his kiss ended several minutes later, she had to rest her head on his chest to catch her breath. His heart thundered under her ear.

"So how many kids would you like to have?"

Her heart skipped a beat. "I always thought a couple would be nice."

"A couple would be very nice," he agreed easily, his hands moving up and down her back. "Have you thought of a date yet?"

"No, but you're right. I don't want it to be too far away, maybe about two months."

"I can agree with that if you can. Shall we go look at schedules then call your parents? I was wondering about driving out to meet them next weekend after the soccer game."

"That would be wonderful. Thank you."

ⓒ𝔰𝔟𝔬

"Toby, I need you to talk to me. I need you to tell me about Sandra."

"I like Sandra. She is my friend. I didn't hurt her, I promise. And I wouldn't hurt Jillian. I didn't mean for her to fall." He looked as if he was about to cry. "I shouldn't have yelled at her. Is she mad at me?"

"No. She's not mad."

"Why didn't she come to see me then?"

"She wanted to, but I asked her to let me talk to you first, and she had to go to work. Will you answer my questions? Your mother said it was all right if you talked to me."

He nodded. "She told me to talk to you. She said you would stop asking questions if I asked you to. That you would be nice and not get mad at me."

"That's right. She said you didn't want her in here. She can be in here if you want."

"Uh, she's been crying. I don't like to see her cry." He looked downcast.

"It's all right, Toby." Mark tried to calm him. It was hard not to feel like an ogre when the man looked so helpless. He knew it was no act. He was like a little boy. Jordan was much more mature than Toby. Mark couldn't help thinking how he would feel if Jordan was in that chair.

The only thing was, if Toby went out of control, Toby had the strength to take out a couple guys before they could get him restrained. He had the sore ribs to remind him of that. Bottom line, he had trouble seeing Toby killing women.

Jillian was right. It just didn't seem to be in his personality, but what if there was another personality in there? He'd talked to Toby's mother for quite some time, and she was certain there wasn't. It just didn't add up. Toby was following Jillian. There was no doubt on that, but still.

"Toby, why are you following Jillian? We found pictures in your car of her."

"I like to take pictures of her. She's beautiful. She smells nice too."

Mark could agree with that.

"And she's always nice to me. I guess maybe I shouldn't have taken pictures of her without asking. But, I liked having them. I have pictures of Sandra, too."

"Yes, I know, we found them."

"She knew I took them. She posed for me."

"Okay. Toby, will you tell me about the book?"

"What book?" He looked up at him, then to Andrew standing in the corner.

"The book of Beauty and the Beast we found in your car."

"I didn't steal it. It was sitting on my car yesterday morning when I came out. I didn't know whose it was. It didn't have a library sticker on it, so it wasn't a library book. I looked. I put it in the car so the sprinklers didn't get it wet. I was going to ask the other kids if they lost it, but I didn't get back to."

"So it was just sitting on your car?"

He nodded. "Yes."

"Did you read it?"

This time he shook his head. "No. I know the story. Mom used to read it to me. And we have the movie."

"You like the story?"

He nodded.

"But, you didn't read it." Mark pressed for an answer.

"I didn't. I promise I was going to give it back." His look was full of remorse.

"All right, I've got to go now. Do you need anything?" He found himself asking.

"Can I get some more breakfast?" Toby looked hopeful.

"I'll see what I can do." He studied him a second before walking out of the room.

Andrew followed him. "What do you think?"

"If I go with my gut, I think he's telling the truth." Mark went over everything in his mind, and it still just didn't add up that Toby was the killer. Looking back at his second in command, he put the question to him. "What do you think?"

"I'm in agreement. That isn't an act in there, and I don't think he has it in him to avoid leaving evidence and not getting caught sooner."

"But, if it isn't him, then the real killer is close enough to know Toby hangs around Jillian, to use him to throw us off the trail."

"You going to release Toby?"

Mark paused to think. "No, I want to get the lab results back first. Toby said he didn't read the book. Let's see where his prints show up. If they're all over the pages, then he lied to us. But, if they're only on the cover and a few pages inside −" he let it hang, but Andrew caught on the same line of thought.

"You think the only fingerprints we'll find are Toby's?" It was more a statement than question.

"Yeah, I do. It's too neat and tidy for Toby to have it there in the car like that. I don't like it." Mark grew thoughtful again.

"I could play devil's advocate for a while and ask you if it's not just wishful thinking for your fiancée."

"You could but you won't because you agree with me."

"Yup. The blood type is the same but so is a lot of the population. I think when the DNA tests come back we'll have proof Toby's innocent."

"Which means the killer may still be after Jillian. I'm going to head over to her shop and check on her." The sentence was barely out when his phone rang. Mark looked at the caller ID and bit back a groan. "Hang on a minute, it's the mayor."

He answered the call and was even less happy when it ended. "I've got to go over to the mayor's office for a minute. Someone leaked that we have a suspect in custody, and they called a press conference. There's supposed to be someone with Jillian."

"Right, I'll double check to make sure we've got a man on that. Then I'll have someone get Toby some more breakfast and go down to the lab and see if they have anything yet on the book or if I can hurry them along."

"Thanks. Give me a call as soon as you hear."

"You really are worried."

"I don't think we have a lot of time. If it's not Toby, the guy will have to know it won't fool us long. Then we'll be back after him."

"You want me to bring Jillian in?"

Andrew's comment went with what Mark was

thinking. He knew Jillian wouldn't like it, but maybe it was time. "No, I'll give her a call now and stress not to go anywhere without the officer, and as soon as I'm done at the press conference, I'll head over there."

He set off down the hall, bringing up Jillian's number. "Jillian." He felt a wave of relief when she answered.

"How's Toby?"

He smiled at her greeting. "He's fine. They're just getting him his second breakfast."

"You don't think it's him?" She sounded satisfied.

"It's still out," he said, not that it seemed to do any good.

"You don't. I love you." There was no missing the warmth in her tone that came over the line.

"I love you, too," he said in a low voice, not breaking his stride. "Do me a favor. I've got another press conference right now. Then I'm heading over there. Promise me, if you have to go anywhere, and I mean anywhere, even to take out the garbage, take the officer on duty. You got it?" He winced at the forcefulness in the words.

"Mark." There was a tremor in her voice now.

"Just promise me." He reached the parking lot and waited for her answer.

"I promise."

"Good, I'll give you a call as soon as the conference is over. Love you." It felt good voicing the words and hearing her return them before disconnecting. His car was right there. He had to force himself to walk past it toward the city building. He could see the group of reporters already gathered.

◌৪◌

Jillian slipped the phone in her pocket and felt a wave of unease. Mark was worried. He hadn't even bothered to hide it.

"Hey, Cherry Blossom, something wrong?" Nan's

voice cut in her thoughts.

Jillian jerked a little. "Oh, no."

"Don't tell me you scared him at how fast we're moving on setting things up."

The smile crept back to Jillian's lips. "I didn't get to tell him. He was on his way to a press conference."

"He said he wanted soon, and you two did agree on the date, Sugar Plum."

This time, the shiver that went through her was one of excitement. Looking at their schedules, they'd picked a date just eight weeks away. The shortness of the time frame seemed staggering, but since she'd arrived at the shop this morning, Nan and her mother had been on the phone and computer sending things back and forth.

They had already lined up the location and caterer. They were now flashing up picture of dresses for bridesmaids and tuxes to give her ideas. She and Mark had an appointment for pictures early Saturday morning. She made a mental note to make sure he could make it.

She also had an appointment to look at dresses Monday morning with her mother and flowers in the afternoon with the florist she favored. She couldn't believe all that had been accomplished in a couple of hours. All the while, she was trying to get some work done.

She turned back to the order form she was filling out when the phone rang again.

"Taylored Designs, this is Jillian Taylor."

"Yeah, Miss Taylor."

Jillian strained to hear the caller. The voice sounded very nasally and muffled on the phone. "I'm helping Ryan Stoddard at the Van Buren Mansion, and he found something he wanted you to have a look at right away. He was wondering if you could come right out."

She glanced at her watch. Mark said he was coming over right after the press conference, but that would take at least a good hour, she was sure. That should give her plenty of time. She just hoped it wasn't anything serious. "I can be there in about fifteen minutes," she said, and the phone cut off in her ear.

She grabbed up her tote with her tape measures and sketch pads, and glanced back over her desk if she needed anything else and decided she didn't. Since she wasn't driving, there was no reason to worry about her purse. "Nan, I have to run over to the Van Buren place. It shouldn't take long."

Nan's quick "So long," reached her as she went through the back door. The police car was parked where it had been earlier. She pulled open the door and slid in the seat.

"Do you mind if we take a drive?" she said, placing her tote on the floor.

"That's fine."

She froze at the voice. Slowly, she turned. She knew the officer sitting there, but it wasn't the officer who had dropped her off. "Detective Crocker." A shot of unease ran through her.

Chapter Fifteen

"Where is Officer Brown?" Jillian knew the question came out sounding rude, but the thought of spending more than half an hour with the distasteful man put her on edge.

"He had an emergency. One of his kids had his appendix burst. They've taken him into surgery. I'm the replacement. Where would you like to go?"

For a moment, Jillian contemplated getting back out of the car, then she remembered she might have her own emergency on her hands, and she'd promised Mark she wouldn't go anywhere without a guard. She closed the door. "The Van Buren mansion. Do you know where it is?"

"Sure."

Silence filled the car as he pulled out on the road. Jillian fought to keep herself from fidgeting in the seat. She jumped when his voice broke the tomb-like atmosphere in the car.

"You're redoing that old derelict?"

"Yes." Her voice cracked. "And, it's not a derelict. It's a great, historical structure. It will be beautiful."

Silence returned to the car, only to be broken again by Crocker. "Look, I owe you an apology. The other day, I was out of line, both times. I shouldn't have said the things

I did. It was wrong. I really don't believe that it was …
well, it's not the victim's fault. I was just … you look kind
of like … I lost someone recently. You remind me of her."
The choked quality in the man's voice brought tears to
Jillian's eyes.

"I'm sorry." They weren't just words. She ached for
the man as pain waved through the car.

"She was so good. I couldn't understand what she saw
in me, but she loved me. It's not fair. I couldn't save her.
I'm supposed to protect." The words broke off.

"It's not your fault." Jillian brushed at the tear that
etched its way down her cheek. "You can't stop all the bad
things. They happen. They shouldn't, but they do." She
tried to swallow back the other tears that threatened. "You
say I remind you of her. Well, if she is like me, she
wouldn't want you to blame yourself. If you could have
stopped it, you would have. You are a protector, but you
can't save everyone."

"That's what the shrinks have been telling me. And I
understand that but−"

Jillian knew he was thinking he still failed. "It doesn't
make it any easier."

"No, it doesn't, but I wanted to say I was sorry. I took
what I was feeling out on you." The man kept his focus
straight forward, but there was no denying the depth of his
sincerity. The tension that had invaded her body since
getting in the car dissipated. By the time they pulled into
the mansion drive a couple minutes later, she felt relaxed
around the man.

"I thought you were to meet someone here?" Crocker
asked, not seeing any cars in front.

"I am. He must be parked around back by the kitchen
entrance, but here in front will be easiest for you to park.
There are a lot of materials that have been unloaded in
back."

Crocker pulled up to the massive front steps and cut

the engine. He was around the car before Jillian got the tote out of the way. "Here let me take that." He reached for the bag.

"Thanks." She handed it over so she could stand. "It's not too heavy, just bulky. I tend to carry a lot of stuff in it. I never know when I'm going to have to mark, measure, or draw up something, so it always pays to be ready."

"Are you redoing the whole mansion?"

"Yes, top to bottom." Excitement washed through her as they went up the stairs. "It's a dream job. I was fortunate to get it."

Jillian tested the door handle and was surprised when it actually turned. The foyer was empty except for the scaffolding and heavy drop cloths covering the floor. "You know," she turned back to the detective, "if you want to give me the bag and go back and sit in the car that won't bother me. There really isn't anywhere to sit in here."

"That's okay. I'd like to have a look around if you don't mind?"

"Not at all. It's a fascinating house. I'm going to head back to the kitchen. That's where we've been having the most challenges."

Jillian took the tote bag and started to weave her way back through the old mansion, having to work around several areas that had been blocked off for construction. Finally, she switched direction to cut across the ballroom to head to the kitchen. The heels of her shoes echoed on the hardwood floor.

She paused to survey the room. It seemed so oppressive. Only wisps of light with dust particles flickering in them made it past the drawn drapes. The heavy material that had once been blue had faded to a dull grayish tone. Still, in her mind, she brought up the picture of how it would look once it was restored. It would be spectacular with the chandelier gleaming over the highly polished, inlaid, wood floor.

She would come to the opening gala with Mark. He would be her husband then, and he would dance her around the room. It would be like a fairy tale.

Love me, Beauty. She recoiled as the words came to her mind. Nausea crept up on her. She pushed it down and continued across the room. The swinging door creaked as she went through it making a shiver scamper down her spine.

"Ryan." Her voice echoed, and her brows furrowed at the empty room. She turned and listened, but there was no sound to lead her to the contractor. Confused, she went to the door to check for his truck. Unlike the front door handle, this one refused to turn when she twisted it. She fought to release the lock, but it wouldn't budge. Well, she'd have to get Ryan to fix that, though she was sure that was not the reason he called her here. She turned to look for signs of the man, but nothing looked different from when she'd been there the day before.

An eerie silence draped over her. Never before had she noticed how tomb-like the old, hulking structure seemed.

"Oh, man." She laughed at herself, talking out loud. "I'm getting paranoid." The words shifted to a small screech when a crash sounded from the front of the house. She placed a hand over her heart as she drew in a deep breath, then let out the air, steadying herself. Well, at least, she now knew where Ryan was. She headed in the direction, choosing again to cut through the ballroom. This time, she walked on her toes to keep her heels from clacking on the wood.

"Love me, Beauty."

The words came at her again only this time they were not in her mind. They were loud and clear and coming from the inside of the room. Jillian spun toward the window at the figure that appeared through the shadows. A dark cloak swirled melodramatically around his body. The hideousness of the snarling, animal-like mask made her gasp, but it was the hand reaching out to her that filled her with terror.

"Dance with me, Beauty."

"No." The word barely made it out as a whisper.

He stepped toward her. She involuntary moved back as if they were indeed in some kind of dance. "Love me, Beauty."

Jillian screamed, backing farther away.

The Beast shook his head. "No, Beauty." His words cut through her. "You are mine."

The icy certainty in the words spurred her to action. She ran back toward the kitchen. "Ryan! Detective Crocker!"

His laughter reached out as he moved to cut her off. "There's no one to hear you. It's just you and me in our castle, as it should be. You will love me, Beauty."

"No," she screamed again as he closed in. She swung the tote she still held. It caught him in the side with a surprising amount force, ripping the bag from her fingers. He staggered back and went down. She spun and ran for the front of the house.

CB&ED

Mark stood off to the side looking out over the crowd that had gathered. He shook his head in annoyance. The mayor hadn't even listened when he tried to tell him he was certain that they had the wrong man. The phone in his pocket rang, and he reached for it in partial defiance for the proceedings going on at the microphone.

"What do you have for me?" he answered seeing Andrew's name on the caller ID.

"The lab guys got the book done. It wasn't hard. It was pretty much how you thought. The book had been wiped clean. The few prints on the cover and a few pages were Toby's. Though they did find a couple of smudges of partials on a couple pages that didn't look the same but not clear enough to run them. They said they could possibly match them up if we have a different suspect."

"Good. It doesn't quite clear him. But it's enough for me, for now."

"Wait." The man cut in before he hung up.

"What?"

"I should've started with this. While waiting, I was looking over the stuff they laid out that was found in his car. There was a receipt there for the pictures taken of Jillian. The date caught my eye. They were paid for and picked up the same time Tina Kimball was murdered, almost two miles away. Toby couldn't have done it."

Mark released a breath, so Toby was cleared. Jillian would be happy to hear that. "Good work, thanks." Mark hung up with all intention to call her but was just in time to hear the mayor announce him.

Frustrated, he stepped to the microphones, nodding to the crowd. "I know you all came here expecting good news, that we have the killer in custody. Unfortunately, I have to say that is not the case. The man we have in custody has been cleared. I want to take this time to tell the women, especially those fitting the victim profile, to use caution. Do not go out alone and always be aware of your surroundings. We are putting all our effort into finding this killer. We do have several leads we are following but, until he's caught, please use care. Thank you." He stepped back, ignoring the buzz going through the crowd until a shout rose over the rest.

"Chief Richards, is it true you're engaged?"

Mark paused, looking back at the reporter. "That has nothing to do with this."

"Then it's true." Another reporter said.

After a moment's hesitation, Mark sighed and stepped back to the microphones. It would come out sooner or later, and maybe they just needed something positive in all the turmoil. "It has nothing to do with this, but yes, I'm engaged to Jillian Taylor, a local interior designer. We're getting married in a couple months."

It was an excited ripple that went through the crowd this time. "When did you get engaged? How did you meet?" The questions rang up from the crowd.

He raised his hand for quiet. "That's it for now."

The mayor was red-faced when he approached him. "What is this that you don't have the killer?"

"We don't. I tried to tell you that."

"You didn't say it was positive before."

"I got the confirmation just before going on the stand. Our suspect's been cleared."

The mayor started to say something more just as Mark's phone rang. Mark reached for it, looking at the number. "Sorry, mayor, I have to take this. It might be important." Mark didn't believe it was, but he wanted an excuse to get away from the man. "Richards."

☙❧

"Beauty" the haunting moan trailed after her as she dodged around the corner, nearly stumbling over debris on the floor. Coming to a blocked off area, she dodged into a small parlor. Ahead, the crossbars of the scaffolding were visible. Behind her, she could hear the heavy footsteps as The Beast pursued her. They weren't hurried, just an even steady drumming on the floor.

Jillian grabbed one of the pieces of metal tubing of the scaffold and swung under it, then climbed over the next. Her jacket caught on a piece of metal. She pulled, tearing the jacket, and fell to floor, crawling the rest of the way until out.

The second she was clear, she was on her feet, running the last few steps to the door. This time, when she grabbed the handle it failed to turn in her hand. She pulled with added fear spurring her on. Frustration burst in her, and she slammed her hand against the solid mahogany. "Help!" she cried, wondering where the detective was.

"Beauty." The words wafted out at her.

With one last smack, she broke away from the door, heading down the other hall toward the library and the doors leading out from there. The way down this side of the house was clearer, and she picked up speed, sprinting for the door at the end of the hall.

She slowed to open the door, then ducked through. Caution hit her mind, and she closed it quietly. Turning, she stumbled over a mound on the floor, and she went down. A barely audible groan escaped the man she landed on.

"Detective Crocker!" She reached for him, then pulled her hand back at the sight of blood pooling around his body. Rolling him slightly on his side revealed the gash in his sport coat.

The gasp died in her throat as the other words reached her.

"Beauty, come to me, my Beauty."

"No." Jillian fought down the cry and pushed herself up, diving for the door. Her hand trembled as she managed to turn the old locking mechanism.

She went back to the detective. Her heart pounded, but she began to think more clearly. Help was the first thing her mind locked on. They needed help. She patted down the detective's pockets looking for a cell phone since hers was in the tote back on the ballroom floor.

When she found no phone and his gun holster empty, she knew The Beast had taken them. That meant he had a gun. Not that she figured he'd use it on her – no, on her he would use his knife. Shuddering, terror rose within.

Jillian forced it down. Now was not the time to panic. It was time to think.

Help – they had to have help, but she couldn't leave Detective Crocker. The way he was bleeding, he wouldn't survive long. She pulled off her jacket, wrapped the body of it to make a wad, and then worked it under his sport coat over the wound. She used the sleeves to tie it into to place.

A weak gasp escaped him as she tightened it down.

"I'm sorry," she whispered.

Satisfied it was the best she could do, she was left with getting him somewhere safe. There was no doubt that if The Beast found him still alive, he would finish killing him. Jillian moved to the bookcase and ran her hand along the shelf to find the hidden lever. Touching it, she pushed and was rewarded with a faint click. Thank heavens for Ryan's fascination with the secret doors. The first thing he did was to oil and get them working.

Detective Crocker was a solidly built man. It took all her strength just to drag him into the passageway. His body left a trail in the dust on the floor. Jillian only hoped The Beast wouldn't know how to open the panel or would be more concerned in following her than going after the injured detective.

Jillian closed the panel firmly, shutting the detective in, and ran to the French doors. Flipping the latch, she gripped the handles, turned and pulled. The doors only shifted about a half-inch. That was when she saw the chain through the window. It was wrapped around the handles and locked in place. She knew then why the other doors wouldn't open. He'd sealed her in.

She thought about smashing the glass, but then there were the chains. Besides, the first thing Mrs. Van Buren had wanted done was to have all the windows, broken and otherwise, replaced with triple pane, tempered glass so no one could break in and destroy things once the work had begun. It was a great idea, but she wasn't likely to be able to put her hand through it.

Across the room, the door handle rattled. Jillian spun to face it, her hand going to her mouth to keep back the cry that tried to escape. "Beauty." The name seeped through the door. "Come to me, Beauty. You are my one."

"That's what you think," she said to herself in a hushed voice. Crossing the floor as silently as possible to the other wall, she opened another panel. This one had a flight of stairs going up.

Something slammed on the door. She jerked around just as a roar split the air from behind the door. She didn't know how long it would hold, but another blow spurred her into the dark stairwell with a prayer that The Beast didn't know about the secret passages. She closed the panel and plunged into inky darkness.

Her breath caught as she fought to steady her nerves. The passage was narrow. With her hands out on both sides touching the walls, Jillian climbed. The sounds of dulled thuds and another roar could barely be heard. One step in front of the other, she made her way up, wishing she had her flashlight, which like her cell-phone, it was in her tote.

Fear spiked again when she reached the top and couldn't see to find the catch to open the exit. For a moment, she was tempted just to wait there until Mark came to find her. He would come looking for her. She had no doubt of that.

He'd said he was coming by after the press conference. How long ago was that? Maybe, forty minutes ago. She could hide here for that long. But what if the conference went longer? There was also the time for him to get to her studio and find out she was missing and get here. It could be hours. She could wait that long, but Detective Crocker couldn't. He needed help, now.

Jillian tried to picture the location of the lock in her mind. She had been through this way several times. With her hand at about waist height, she ran her fingers over the wall until she found the barely discernible seam. Inching her hand slightly to the right, she traced it up and down until she felt the indentation.

With a deep intake of air, she held her breath and pressed. In the tomb-like silence, the click sounded thunderous. She glanced down the stairs. When there was no answering movement at the bottom, she pulled open the door and eased through.

ᄊᅍ

"Mark," Edward Samuelson's voice reached out to him from the phone. "I think we may have something on the flowers."

"Tell me." His body shifted to full alert.

"We've been looking for the florists in the area that carry American Beauty roses. There are only a couple. And, since some people pay with cash, our list had quite a few holes in it, but I think I just got lucky. I talked to a lady who, when I asked about American Beauties specifically, she remembered something odd happened about three weeks ago. A man came in and requested a bouquet of American Beauty roses. He was very specific she said. She'd sold out and offered him another variety. He became irate. He insisted they had to be American Beauties."

Mark felt his heart jump as Edward kept talking. "The man had her find out who else in the area handled them, then call to make sure they had them. When she asked for a name to have them held under, he refused to give it."

"Did you get a description?" Mark had to know now.

"I got better than that. After the guy left, the woman kept thinking about him. She knew she'd seen him before. Later, she got a call from a friend, and it dawned on her where she'd seen him. Her friend works at the newspaper and she'd been there visiting her. It was Nigel Clark."

The air caught in Mark's chest, and he turned to scan the crowd of reporters. Clark wasn't there. He hadn't seen him the whole time, which was unusual because Clark was the one covering the killings. He was always there.

"Get an APB out on Clark. I want him brought in for questioning right now," he growled out the last word. A wave of certainty burned in him. Clark was the killer. He looked over the reporters one more time. Why wasn't he there? Where could he be?

Ice filled his insides. Disengaging the call, he scanned

until he spied the reporter from the same paper. People parted out of his way as he strode through the crowd.

"Where's Clark?"

His demand took the man by surprise, and he stumbled over the answer. "He ... he called in sick today."

Mark didn't wait for anything else. He turned, moving away from the crowd. He broke into a run, pressing the dial to Jillian as his long stride ate up the ground to the parking lot. It rang and rang with no answer. He hung up and pressed another number. Nan's voice answered, "Taylored Designs," just as he slid into his car.

"Where's Jillian?" He barked out, urgency to hear her voice pumped in him.

"She went out to the Van Buren mansion." Nan's voice quivered in response, obviously sensing something was wrong.

"When did she leave?" He flipped on his flashing lights.

"Right after she talked to you. She went with the officer."

"If she calls, have her call me."

"What's wrong?"

He heard the woman asking as he cut the connection, punching another button, while pressing down on the accelerator.

"Dispatch."

"This is Chief Richards, find out who's escorting Jillian Taylor and connect me." He forced himself to slow and gripped the wheel to make a turn.

The wait was unbearable before the voice came back on line. "Detective Crocker is attached to Jillian Taylor, but there's no answer on either his unit or phone. Sir, one of the other dispatchers just had a call come in from Detective Crocker's phone. The call was cut off. All we got was what sounded like a request to send back up before the line went dead. They've been trying to locate him."

"Send units to the Van Buren mansion. You'll have to look up the address. Also, have Andrew Hamilton and Edward Samuelson meet me there."

He dropped the phone in his lap as he took another corner, praying his fears were all for nothing but knowing inside that Jillian was in danger.

ᏃᎬᎧ

Jillian's heart pounded as she stood inside what had been the master bedroom. Relieved to be out of the darkness, she was uncertain what to do next. She strained to hear any sounds from below. There were none. Deathly quiet seemed to invade the building. She wished she knew where The Beast was or what she should do. Getting out was the simplest, most logical thing.

A floorboard creaked on the first step she took and she froze. Taking a deep breath she tried again, this time cautiously placing her weight down and was rewarded with silence. Reassured, she continued her way across the room toward the doors leading to the balcony. She froze with each sound, afraid that any minute The Beast would burst through the door.

Jillian was only a few feet from the doors when she saw the chains. She wanted to scream or cry. Instead, she shifted directions to the hall. With one hand on the handle, the other on the door in case she needed to slam it shut, she turned the knob and eased it open, praying it wouldn't creak. There was only a slight sound, but it made her insides clinch.

Holding her breath, she peeked around the doorframe. The hall was empty. Still she waited before moving out, trying to come up with a plan. All the rooms on this side of the mansion had French doors that led out onto the balcony. She had no doubt they would all be chained.

On the other side, the rooms had windows that looked out over the front drive. She couldn't think of a way he could seal them, unless he nailed them shut. The problem there was she'd be faced with a fifteen foot drop. If she clung to the sill and lowered herself down, it would only be about ten feet. She should be able to do that. She just hoped she didn't sprain an ankle or break a leg. Still, it was better than facing The Beast.

Jillian had only taken three steps out into the hall when she heard a floorboard near the top of the massive circular staircase squeak. Terror pushed her forward. She'd just started for the door when he spoke.

"Beauty, why do you run from me? We are meant to be together. You will save me from the beast I've become." The words were filled with madness. The haunting cadence was sickening.

She grabbed the handle and shoved at the door. Stumbling into the room, she slammed the door behind her. Jillian turned to lock it and cried out. The lock was broken. A quick scan showed there was nothing in the room she could use as a weapon so she dove for the window. It was doubtful she'd make it but she wasn't going to give up without trying.

This time the lock turned in her hand, and the window slid open easily. Jillian sat on the sill and draped one leg over just as the door burst open. The blast of it bouncing off the wall echoed in the room. Jillian grabbed the edge to propel herself over as the figure leapt across the room, his cloak billowing out around him like massive black wings.

Jillian pushed off the sill just as the hand locked around her wrist. She swung down but her body slammed into the siding, knocking the breath from her. The muscles in her shoulder screamed, and the sound followed it out of her mouth.

Agony swept over her. She thought her arm would be ripped from its socket. Lights swirled in front of her eyes. Jillian wondered if she blacked out for a minute because, the next thing she knew, she was being dragged over the ledge.

"Beauty."

The Beast was bending over her again, just like he had the first night and again in her nightmares.

A whimper escaped her.

He stroked back her hair. "I have you, Beauty."

Jillian shook her head in the negative, unable to get words past her lips.

The roar that erupted from behind the mask was almost inhuman. "Love me, Beauty!" The words gnashed out.

Too many times the words had haunted her, and her soul rebelled at hearing them again. "No!" she screamed, throwing her hands up, clawing at the face behind the mask with her own animalistic instinct.

The arms holding her released their grip. Her hand locked on the mask pulling it with her as she dropped to the floor, not lessening her attack. She kicked out and hit, ignoring the pain in her shoulder.

A snarl, like some feral animal exploded from the figure. She looked up at the man. The face without the mask or wig was hardly less beastly. His scalp was covered with roughened, discolored skin, but it was the expression that frightened her. His lips were pulled back. In his madness, saliva seeped from the corners. His eyes were wild with the hatred that burned in them. The familiar features of the reporter were barely discernible in the twisted fury of The Beast.

Shock at realizing who it was faded under the reality that he was going to kill her.

CR8O

Mark sped up the hill, taking the curve faster than was safe. The mansion came into view in front of him. He felt a wave of relief at seeing the building until he noticed movement at an upstairs window. He was close enough to make out Jillian. His stomach clenched as she put her leg over the ledge, and he realized she was going to jump.

He was hardly able to force his concentration back to

the road long enough to make it through the gates, then it went right back to the window as Jillian's body dropped. Instead of falling, she swung out, then slammed into the side of the building, and Mark saw the monstrous shape holding her.

His hand went to his gun as he skidded to a stop behind two other police cars. In one motion he was out of the car and had his gun up but halted, unable to take the shot with Jillian being pulled back through the window blocking his view of The Beast.

Mark ran for the mansion, joined by another officer.

"All the doors are chained and padlocked," the officer informed him, holding up a pair of bolt cutters which he had just taken from his trunk.

"Get it open!" Mark ordered, his attention going back to the window. There was no sign of Jillian now, but her scream echoed down, cutting through him.

It seemed an eternity, though only about three seconds for the cutters to bite through the chain. Mark joined the officer in freeing the knob and pulled the door open. He took the stairs three at a time with the officers right behind him. The sounds of struggling led him to the room. With his gun out in ready position, he burst around the corner.

Jillian was on the floor at the killer's feet. Nigel Clark held her up by her hair, the knife raised over her.

"Clark!" Mark yelled.

The man froze, his attention shifting up. "She's mine!" Clark snarled, plunging the knife down toward her. The blast from Mark's gun hit him in the shoulder driving him back. Jillian ripped away and rolled to the side just as a howl burst from The Beast.

Clark charged at Mark, slashing out with the knife. Mark fired again. The reporter's body jerked with the impact of the bullet but kept coming.

Mark stumbled back into the hall for more space and fired again. His shot was echoed by two more blasts from the other officers.

The Beast made it another step before he staggered and dropped to his knees. "Beauty." The word gurgled from his lips as he fell forward, lifeless.

Jillian appeared in the doorway. Mark opened his arms and caught her as she rushed to him. Pulling her into his chest, he locked his arms over her. It was almost hard to believe that she was there, safe, but her heart thundered in beat with his. She gasped against him, shivers shaking her body.

He pressed his lips into her hair, his own body trembled at how close he came to losing her. He eased her back to rain kisses down on her face. When he would've pulled her into a hug, she shook her head, taking in a deep, shaky breath.

"Detective Crocker," she burst out. "He's hurt bad, in the panel, in the library."

"It's okay." Mark looked over her shoulder at the officer who had been checking the body. "Call for an ambulance." His gaze shifted back to Jillian. "Where?"

She turned. Her breath caught at the sight of the man on the floor.

"Don't look." Mark pulled her into him, blocking her view as he moved her to the stairs.

By the time they made it to the bottom of the stairs, the sound of other sirens approaching could be heard. Jillian clung to him, almost stoically calm, though her hand trembled as she opened the panel. Mark hated to release her but dropped to his knees beside the detective. Seeing the amount of blood, he feared Crocker would be dead, but there was a steady pulse.

Voices and footsteps sounded in the hall. "In here," he yelled, and was joined a second later by the paramedics. "Let's get him out of here." He stepped around to the back of the recess to help lift Crocker out onto the stretcher so the man and woman could go to work. Since there was nothing else he could do for the detective, he returned to Jillian.

"Is he going to be all right?" Her voice trembled. "It was all I could think of to try to stop the bleeding."

Mark watched one paramedic remove her jacket. The other was ready to cut away the shirt and apply a pressure bandage. "You did perfect." He tightened his hold, thinking of her taking the time to try to save the man while fleeing from a killer.

A second later, Andrew walked up to them. "Chief." He drew their attention. "It looks like you got The Beast this time."

"Yeah, is Edward here?"

"Upstairs."

"Get him so you can take our statements. I want to get Jillian out of here as soon as possible."

They were waiting for the detectives on the front steps when the paramedics brought Detective Crocker out. Mark was surprised and relieved to see he was conscious under the oxygen mask. As he passed, he saw his hand came up a little, and he mumbled something. Mark held the paramedics up, bending down to Cocker. Jillian followed suit.

"Saved you."

The raspy words were barely discernible through the mask, but the meaning was clear. He couldn't save the woman he loved but tried to save her.

Tears rushed to her eyes. "Yes, thank you."

The man relaxed visibly. His eyes closed, and they continued to the ambulance.

Jillian stood, leaning back against Mark, wrapped in his arms while watching the vehicle pull away, lights flashing. "He's finally started to forgive himself for not being there to save her."

"It's still going to take him time." He pressed a kiss to her neck. "I don't know what I would have done if I hadn't gotten here in time." Agony dripped from his words and he turned her in his arms. "When I saw you go out that window and then when he stood over you with that knife. I've never been so scared."

"I'm fine. You saved me." She raised a hand to stroke his cheek.

"Yes, this time The Beast didn't win."

"Does that mean you get the happily ever after?"

"Yes." He ignored the people milling around to capture her lips in a kiss, staking a claim that she was his forever.

Epilogue

No fairytale could have been so wonderful. No castle so beautiful. Jillian looked around the ballroom with satisfaction. Perfect. She'd heard that word numerous times that night to describe the mansion, along with amazing, spectacular, breath-taking, and other favorable comments. All true. Everything came together better than she'd even imagined.

It was almost hard to believe that it could have been the same room she'd run through in terror, trying to avoid The Beast. It had taken some time before she could enter it without a touch of fear, even though she knew there was no Beast lurking in the shadow. Her unease lingered until the old faded curtains had been taken down and the floor refinished to its past beauty.

Tonight, all shadows were gone, chased away by the glittering light from the three massive chandeliers hanging from the gleaming inlaid ceiling. Music filled the room along with waves of conversation. Fragrant air drifted in through the row of French doors which opened onto the terrace, keeping the packed room from becoming oppressively hot. The gala was as great a success as the mansion.

So much had changed in five months. The old mansion was now a celebrated jewel of the community. The Beast was a thing of the past. Sandra had fully recovered, as had Detective Crocker and they were now dating. Jillian shook her head at the notion, happy for them.

A shiver ran through her, but it held no tendrils of fear. She turned and heat flared in her at the sight of the handsome man cutting through the crowd toward her. Mark looked as great in a tux as the day they got married.

Even after three months it was hard to believe he was her husband. Life couldn't get any better. They'd blended into the family she thought they were always meant to be. Her heart swelled, remembering how, after they were pronounced husband and wife, he had kissed her, sealing the union. Then she'd turned to Jordan, who'd wrapped his arms around her and hugged her tight.

"Can I call you Mom, now?" He tilted his face up to her.

"Yes." The word brought her as much pleasure as saying it to become the wife of the amazing man who came to a stop three feet away. Longing closed the distance between them.

As if everyone around them could feel it, people parted. Jillian heard several women titter, then lost connection to her surroundings as he spoke.

"May I have this dance?" Mark stretched out his hand.

Jillian placed her fingers lightly in his palm and gasped at the current of awareness. He pulled her into his arms with a smooth move that took her breath.

He nuzzled her cheek. "I'm sorry I got hung up with the mayor. The man can go on forever."

"That's why I snuck away. I was just mingling and admiring my handwork."

"You should be pleased. It's almost as beautiful as you."

"Thank you. I was just thinking it was my own private

fairytale."

He whirled her around. "Does that make me your prince?"

"It does." There was no doubt in her mind.

"So fairytales can come true."

Jillian would've agreed aloud but his mouth settled over hers to seal the truth of it in their hearts.

About the Author

I grew up in a small town in Wyoming loving the outdoors, sports, art, and reading Hardy Boys books. After reading them all at least a half dozen times, I started writing my own stories.

Thirty years ago I married a wonderful, honorable man. I'm mother of five children and grandmother of six boys. I love traveling. Through my husband's work and vacations, I have visited much of the United States, all over Eastern Europe, Canada, Mexico, China, Thailand, Cambodia and Australia, giving me many intriguing locations and experiences for my stories.

I am a storyteller. I write the classic hero story because I think there's a need for more heroes, love, and adventure in our lives. I'm not out to change the world with my writing; I'm just hoping to make your day a little better.

Hope you enjoy.

Alysia S. Knight

Please feel free to visit me through my website:

www.alysiasknight.com